FLINT BOOK 3:
BACK TO THE STREETS

FLINT BOOK 3:
BACK TO THE STREETS

TREASURE HERNANDEZ

www.urbanbooks.net

Urban Books, LLC
78 East Industry Court
Deer Park, NY 11729

Flint Book 3: Back to the Streets Copyright © 2008
Treasure Hernandez

All rights reserved. No part of this book may be repro-
duced in any form or by any means without prior con-
sent of the Publisher, except brief quotes used in
reviews.

ISBN 13: 978-1-60162-293-8
ISBN 10: 1-60162-293-7

First Trade Printing September 2008
First Mass Market Printing October 2010
Printed in the United States of America

10   9   8   7   6   5   4   3   2   1

*This is a work of fiction. Any references or similarities to ac-
tual events, real people, living, or dead, or to real locales are
intended to give the novel a sense of reality. Any similarity in
other names, characters, places, and incidents is entirely coin-
cidental.*

Distributed by Kensington Publishing Corp.
Submit Wholesale Orders to:
Kensington Publishing Corp.
C/O Penguin Group (USA) Inc.
Attention: Order Processing
405 Murray Hill Parkway
East Rutherford, NJ 07073-2316
Phone: 1-800-526-0275
Fax: 1-800-227-9604

R0425695256

Acknowledgments

First and foremost, I would like to thank God for all the blessings he has bestowed upon me.
I would also like to thank all the Urban Books fans for supporting all the creative African American writers.

Please send all letters to Urban Books; they will make sure I get them.

Holla at your girl!!!!

Treasure Hernandez
c/o Urban Books
78 East Industry Court
Deer Park, NY 11729

Love & Peace,

Treasure

Chapter One

Halleigh looked in the mirror and saw a person who bore no resemblance to the young woman she used to be. It seemed like just yesterday she was an excelling senior in high school and dating the most popular boy at school, who just happened to be the biggest up-and-coming basketball star since LeBron James. The two of them had shared champagne dreams of him signing a lucrative NBA contract and then moving the two of them as far away from the city of Flint as possible. But now, more than a year later, she was a highschool dropout, doing something for a living that she never imagined she could ever do.

As Halleigh stood there, her mind wandered off to her first day on the job. She recalled walking through the park hand in hand with Mitch—she'd never forget the name of her first customer. She chuckled at the thought of how people could have mistaken them for longtime lovers instead of the strangers that they were.

They weren't even halfway to Mitch's car when

Halleigh's nerves got the best of her. Her stomach churned, and she felt as though she might throw up. Now that she thought about it, she had thrown up just a little bit, enough where she could swallow it. As nasty as that might sound, she wasn't about to let her customer in on the fact that she had no idea what the fuck she was doing. It might have been her first day on the job, but her customer didn't need to know that.

In the back seat of his ride, an old school song she had heard on the radio by LL Cool J crossed her mind: Back seat of my Jeep, let's swing an episode. So now she was going to learn firsthand just exactly what LL meant—only, her episode was about to take place in the back seat of a 2007 Cadillac Seville.

Sitting in that back seat, she couldn't even remember how she had ended up there. Everything else that followed turned into a blur. Now all Halleigh could remember were two things: the name (Mitch) and the price (two-fifty). Two hundred and fifty dollars is what it had cost her first customer to take ownership of his merchandise, which just happened to be Halleigh herself.

"What happened to me?" Halleigh asked herself. She shook her head in shame as she recalled her recent past. Not only had she been trickin', but to escape the pain and the reality of what she was doing to herself, she added salt to the wounds by pumping drugs into her body.

Before her days of whoring and drugging, her life had been all planned out, and not one of her plans had consisted of being pimped out to the highest bidder. She was supposed to marry Malek—a rising superstar athlete, and her savior—and live happily ever after. She'd wanted it all, everything that being on the arm of an NBA star offered, and was ready to accept her position as Malek's wifey.

Unfortunately, Halleigh's real life didn't live up to her fairytale fantasy. Her life had gone from heaven to hell in the blink of an eye, and she'd had enough. She couldn't take this ghetto-ass lifestyle she had succumbed to.

Halleigh felt the tears flow down her face. They weren't tears of force that came from heaving and overreacting. They were true tears of a broken, hopeless spirit, and they stained her face as she looked down at the gun in her hand.

The day Halleigh copped the gun, she had actually intended to ask her get-high buddy, Scratch, to cop her some heroin. But then, on her way to meet Scratch at their spot in the alley where they had initially met when he tried to rob her with a stick concealed to look like a gun, she noticed how people were looking at her now. She felt as if she were deformed or something, the way they grimaced.

Having been nothing short of a dime-piece, Halleigh was used to turning the heads of gawking men. She was used to the envious glares of women, but this time, the attention she was receiving was different. They were stares of disgust and pity.

As she walked by a used appliance store, she caught a glimpse of her reflection in the window. She stopped in her tracks and gasped at the frail sight before her. Slowly, her hands began to roam her face, just to confirm that the reflection was actually hers. Were those really her eyes she was looking into? Once upon a time those eyes had been full of life and energy, no matter how much negativity they had witnessed.

Halleigh allowed her hands to roam down her body. Wearing tight-fitting jeans with knee-high stiletto boots and a sequined top, she thought she looked just fine, but underneath her hands she could feel almost every bone in her body, every rib. Taking a long, hard look at herself, Halleigh, too, was disgusted by what she saw.

The storeowner interrupted her when he came out of the store and asked if he could help her with anything. Without saying a word, she walked off crying. As far as Halleigh was concerned, what she had just seen wasn't her, but a disintegrating corpse of her former self. She was as good as dead. She felt like death anyway. Hell, she couldn't remember the last time she had felt free and alive. That was the moment she decided she was better off dead than living the way she had been living.

By the time she met up with Scratch, she had a plan all mapped out. As long as Scratch was willing to be her accomplice, she didn't see how the plan could fail.

When she asked Scratch to help her cop a gun, he wasn't for it at first. He was trying to get high with Halleigh's money, not waste it on a cold piece of metal. But after realizing that he could cop a gun and still have money left over to get a hit for himself, he obliged her. She hadn't told him what she intended to do with the weapon. He never asked.

Now, here Halleigh stood in the bathroom of what she called home, which was nothing more than another prison, as far as she was concerned.

Manolo, a.k.a. Daddy, told them when they could leave, when they couldn't, and how long they could stay gone. He needed to know where his money was at all times.

If only I could see the look on that motherfucker's face when he finds me, Halleigh thought with a half-witted smile, the gun to her temple. *His greedy ass probably won't even see my brains splattered all over the walls; he'll see a pile of useless currency.*

Halleigh trembled as the cold steel pressed against her clammy skin. Her body began to break out into a cold, nervous sweat.

Moments from her life flashed before her eyes—all the heartache and tragedy she'd experienced—and she had a drastic decision to make. Live or die? Fight or retreat? Win or lose? She was tired of struggling to survive in a city that had no love for her. She was choosing death, and there was no turning back.

Halleigh put her finger just above the trigger. She squinted her eyes closed tight, and just when she was about to squeeze, there was a knock on the door.

"Hal, what are you doing in there? Open the door!" Mimi's voice came from the other side of the bathroom door, where she stood in the hallway. "You've been in there forever. What's going on?" This was the second time in the past half hour Mimi had knocked on the door to check on Halleigh. She felt as though something wasn't kosher.

Halleigh, who had actually been locked in the small bathroom for the past forty-five minutes, didn't respond.

"Halleigh?" Mimi called again. "Open the door. Why you locking doors around this mu'fucka anyway? You know Manolo will have a fit."

The last time one of Manolo's girls called herself "locking a door," Manolo made it so that she never wanted to be locked up behind a closed door again in her life. For hours Manolo kept her locked inside a dark closet. The girl lost her mind and had to be committed to an institution afterwards. As hard as Mimi had tried to calm the girl down, it was to no avail. Come to find out, the girl's stepfather used to lock her in the closet when she was twelve, but not before running up in her like she was a grown woman.

Mimi had relayed the story to Halleigh, so she hoped Halleigh would take heed and unlock that door with a quickness.

Halleigh's arm shook uncontrollably as Mimi continued knocking. "Just pull the trigger," she whispered to herself. "All of the pain will go away if you just pull the goddamn trigger. Just end it." A small cry escaped her lips. She lowered the gun.

"Halleigh? Are you all right? You crying?" Mimi said, her tone now filled with concern.

"Open the damn door." The fear in her voice translated as if she was angry.

When Halleigh failed to respond, Mimi sensed that something was terribly wrong. "Tasha!" she turned around and yelled. "There's something wrong with Halleigh!"

Wearing only a bra and panties, Tasha appeared from behind her bedroom door. "What do you mean, something's wrong with her?" she asked. With Tasha being in charge of all of Manolo's girls, she was definitely concerned. If anything happened to one of them, she would be the first person Manolo looked to.

"I mean she's in this mu'fucka with the door locked and she's crying and shit." Mimi then began to whisper. "I don't want the bitch to do nothing crazy. You know she just been through all that shit with Malek." Mimi then got an I-told-you-so attitude. "I told y'all she wasn't cut out for this shit."

"Fuck you whispering for? Like she can't hear you." As far as Tasha was concerned, this was not the time for Mimi to be right about her call on Halleigh, especially since Mimi was the one who brought her to the house and got her into the game in the first place.

Tasha came out of her bedroom and walked up to the door. She put her ear against it. She, too, could hear Halleigh whimpering. "Hal, open up the door so we can talk," she urged. She picked up from where Mimi left off and began knocking on the door. "Halleigh, listen, just open up the door." Tasha, her eyes wide with fright, turned around and stared at Mimi.

"I told you," Mimi said, folding her arms pretzel-style. After all the drama and heartache that Halleigh had experienced, Mimi wasn't surprised that she was flipping out. As a matter of fact, the only thing that did surprise her was that she hadn't done it sooner.

In all honesty, Mimi thought that Halleigh wouldn't last after her first trick. But she didn't care, considering she had already gotten her $500 finder's fee for bringing the new girl home.

Halleigh could hear Tasha and Mimi calling for

her, but ignored them. She knew what she had to do, and she wasn't going to let anything distract her from doing it. She lifted the semi-automatic to her head again and cocked it. No matter how hard Halleigh had tried to convince herself over the past few months that things would get better, they hadn't. She felt that shooting her brains out would be a quick end to what felt like a long, miserable life.

Click! Click!

"Oh shit!" Mimi panicked. "Was that a fuckin' gun?"

Before Tasha could reply, they heard loud sounds coming from the bathroom.

Bam!

Mimi and Tasha hit the deck, faces buried in the brown carpet.

"Does that answer your question?" Tasha said to Mimi.

"That crazy bitch is trying to shoot us," Mimi whispered.

After a few seconds of silence, Tasha stood up and pounded her open hand frantically against the door. "Halleigh, if you trying to fuck with our minds, it worked. Now open the damn door!"

There was no reply from the other side.

"Say 'Boo,' fart or do something, damn it. Just at least let us know that you're okay."

That's when it hit Mimi what was really going on. She immediately stood up from the floor. "Oh my God! She shot herself, didn't she?" she asked Tasha. "The broad done shot herself!" Mimi shouted in a panic. "Tasha, do something! Ain't there a key to this motherfucker?" Mimi tried to turn the knob.

Tasha felt helpless. As the madam of the house, she was supposed to keep all of the Manolo Mamis in line. That was why Manolo had appointed her to the job. But, as a woman, Tasha also felt like she was supposed to protect them. She hated the fact that she might not have been able to protect one of the girls from her own self.

Tasha stepped back a couple of feet and mustered up all the strength she had in her body. Next, she charged toward the bathroom door and threw her body against it. When she finally broke it off its hinges, she raced into the bathroom to find Halleigh laid out on the floor with blood behind her head.

"Halleigh, baby girl, what have you done?" Tasha said as she kneeled down next to Halleigh's body.

The moan that was released from Halleigh's lips startled her.

"My head . . ." Halleigh moaned. "I think I hit my head when I fell." Halleigh grabbed the back of her head.

The sound of the gunshot had been deafening as it ricocheted off the bathroom wall. On top of that, the force of pulling the trigger on the weapon had been so great that it knocked Halleigh off her feet and onto the floor.

Tasha didn't know whether to be happy that Halleigh was alive, or pissed that she had scared them half to death. "Fuck is you doing?" Tasha screamed, deciding to be mad. Her shoulder throbbed from the impact of breaking into the bathroom door, but she disregarded the pain as she picked the gun up from the floor and handed it over her shoulder to Mimi.

"Hey, watch how you handling that thing," Mimi said, carefully taking it from Tasha's hand. She then disappeared to get rid of the gun.

Tasha didn't pay Mimi any mind. She focused her attention on Halleigh, who began to shake like a leaf.

Halleigh looked down at the blood on her hand then at the bullet hole in the wall. "I could have . . ." Halleigh hesitated. "I could have . . ." Her cries built up in her throat as she struggled to contain her emotions.

"Shhh. Come here," Tasha said, pulling Halleigh close and comforting her. "It's okay, Hal. Everything is gon' be all right."

After a few moments, Tasha pulled away from Halleigh and looked at her. "I've told you that everything is going to be all right. You just gotta hold on, ma." She put her arms around her friend again and rocked her slowly.

Mimi reappeared at the doorway after burying the gun in a drawer full of lingerie. She looked down at a visibly shaken Halleigh. "Is she all right?" she asked Tasha.

"Yeah, she's okay. She's gon' be fine," Tasha replied, still holding Halleigh tightly.

Mimi was never one to get emotional. The only thing that made her cry was missing out on money, so when Tasha looked up and noticed Mimi's eyes full of tears, she outstretched her other arm to invite Mimi into the embrace. Mimi quickly bent down and filled in the circle and hugged Halleigh as well.

"It's time for this to stop," Tasha stated, her voice cracking. "We can't do this to ourselves anymore. Manolo is the only person getting something out of all this." Tasha looked around. "So he keeps a roof over our heads—We can get that shit on our own." She shook her head. "I can believe we've been selling ourselves short all this time. I mean, he's beaten Hal down to the point where she feels she needs to take her own life. This is bullshit. Nobody should have that much power over us. Nobody!" Tasha had to fight back her own tears. "You and me, Mimi, we're a different breed. We're strong. We can handle this life better than Halleigh, but look at her. Look what this is doing to her."

Mimi nodded.

Tasha shook her head. "First she was trying to kill herself by shooting that shit into her body, and now she's trying to shoot herself, period. This is crazy."

"When black people start killing themselves, oh yeah, you know shit done got too crazy," Mimi agreed.

Halleigh was too distraught to reply. She had just attempted to take her own life—and she might have succeeded if not for the fact that her heroin-wasted muscles couldn't even hold the weight of the gun to aim properly. Otherwise, her two friends would've been weeping over a bleeding corpse. But that's what Halleigh felt like, anyway—dead, and bleeding on the inside.

"I hear what you saying, Tash," Mimi stated, "but you know as well as I do that there ain't no way we leaving Manolo and living to tell about it. Ya heard me?" Mimi stood up. "You already know how he is, Tasha. You've been around longer than any of us. So you tell us what happens when a chick tries to walk away from Manolo."

Tasha relaxed her arms to her side and just swallowed.

"Exactly!" Mimi said, smacking her lips. "So you can give your 'Obama speeches' all day long, telling us what we need to do, but I want you to show me how we're supposed to do it. Tell me, Tasha, how are we supposed to get out of this situation? And if we do make it out, how we gon' survive? All we used to doing is selling pussy. So what's the difference whether we're selling it for ourselves or Manolo? Selling pussy is selling pussy."

Tasha knew that Mimi's words were true. They couldn't just walk away from Manolo without recourse. He was Daddy, and would kill them before he let them leave. And even if she did find a way to pull the girls out from under Manolo's clutches, what would be their means of survival? She was stuck between a rock and a hard place, but that didn't deter her from wanting to escape from Manolo's iron-fisted rule.

"What are we gon' do?" Mimi asked again.

"Let me think. Damn!" Tasha replied, aggravated that she didn't have all of the answers to Mimi's queries. She had never thought this tough about trying to dip out on Manolo, so, no, the answers weren't at the top of her head. But once she thought this thing through clearly, she was sure she'd figure a way out. "For right now, just shut up and help me get Halleigh up from the floor."

Mimi gave her a questioning look, still wanting answers.

Tasha told her, "Look, all I know is that I'm gonna have us out of here by the end of the week, I promise. That's my word."

Upon hearing Tasha's promise, an emotion finally registered on Halleigh's face. It was a look of surprise laced with disbelief.

Tasha noticed Halleigh's expression, and she wanted to remove her doubt. "I promise, Hal," Tasha reaffirmed. She didn't know how she was going to pull it off, but she knew she had to at least try . . . for the sake of them all.

Chapter Two

Tariq sat breaking down the buds of weed on the table as the hustlers that worked for him crowded around. They were listening to him talk mad shit about his superior.

"Fuck Jamaica Joe!" Tariq spat. "I'm the next big thing 'round this mu'fucka." He filled the blunt with the goods, lit it, and continued to put on a show for his crew. "Just stick wit' me and you're gonna go places," he stated.

They were all inside the crack house that Jamaica Joe had assigned Tariq to run. Drug addicts filed in to buy their preferred drug as Tariq sat at the table in the middle of the dope spot. For the past fifteen minutes, he'd been bragging about how he was going to take over the North Side drug game, and how nothing or no one would get in his way.

"Yo, and that ho-ass nigga Malek is done, nah mean? That nigga ain't a hustla anyway. Before Joe took that nigga in, he was a soft-ass ballplayer who didn't know shit about the streets of Flint. Now that nigga think he Rich Porter or somebody. I'm telling you, son, I got some shit about to pop off soon, and when it do pop off, that nigga Joe and Malek are gonna be outta dis bitch. Trust that!" Tariq said, jealousy overtaking his emotions.

For the past week, Tariq had been creating a plan to get Joe and Malek out of the picture. Unfortunately, his last two attempts to set up his former comrade had failed miserably. Tariq had provided Sweets, who ran the South Side and who was also Joe's biggest enemy, inside information on Joe in order to catch him slippin'. Neither time had Sweets been able to take out Joe. This third time, though, had to be a charm, or else Tariq was certain Jamaica Joe would be on to the fact that someone on the inside was setting him up. Since, besides Malek, Tariq was the closest and knew all of Joe's business, it probably wasn't going to take long for the finger to get pointed his way.

But Tariq's level of confidence was up so high, he shook off that thought. Matter of fact, he was so confident that he had no fear in expressing himself, knowing that Jamaica Joe wouldn't be around long enough to find out about it anyway.

Tariq and Jamaica Joe went way back in the street game, always playing on the same team. Until recently, Tariq had always been loyal to his superior, but now, as far as he was concerned, Joe shit on that loyalty thing when he let some punk-ass teen who hadn't put in no work in the streets come in and try to play his position.

As Tariq began to fill one of his closest workers in on the plan to take down Joe, a fiend approached the table, looking to cop a fix. Tariq was in mid-sentence when the fiend interrupted him.

"Excuse me, youngblood. Can I get a dime?" The crackhead stood before Tariq with a handful of quarters, dimes, and pennies.

Tariq slapped the change out of the crackhead's hands, causing all of the coins to scatter across the hardwood floor. The other users scrambled for the change and eventually left the man with only a few cents.

"Didn't you see me over here talking to my mans?" Tariq spat. "Don't interrupt me for a mu'-fuckin' dime rock. You betta go and holla at one of them li'l niggas out front and cop," Tariq said as he watched the man scramble for any of his change that hadn't already been confiscated.

Tariq and the worker he had been discussing his plan with laughed as they watched the fiend walk out of the crackhouse with no money and no drugs, a crackhead's nightmare. Once the fiend left, Tariq continued explaining his plan to take out Jamaica Joe.

By the end of the night, he was high off the bomb weed he had been tootin' and the anticipation that he would soon reign the North Side drug game.

Jamaica Joe and Malek sat in the spacious back seat of the all-black Bentley as they were chauffeured by one of Joe's henchmen. The curtains on the windows hid their faces from the public, but unless they had been under a rock or were new to the city, everyone knew who was inside the luxury vehicle. Typically, they would have been rolling in Joe's black Lincoln Navigator, but that had been riddled with bullets when someone tried to rob him. Unbeknownst to Joe, it had been one of Tariq's failed setups

Malek looked through the back window and then at Joe. "Yo, Joe, I think someone is following us. That car been on us since Ballenger Road," Malek said in reference to the blue Ford Taurus with tinted windows behind them.

"Ah, don't worry about them. That's just the Feds," Joe said nonchalantly. "They been on me for the last couple of weeks. But I ain't pressed. They don't have anything on a nigga. They're just waiting for me to slip up. But it ain't gon' happen, feel me?" Joe didn't even look back once. Everything about him reflected that he wasn't the least bit worried. It showed in his actions and the tone of his voice. He knew that the FBI were on him closely, and he understood that the war he had with the South Side and Sweets was what brought the attention his way.

"Damn, fam, it's like that?" Malek couldn't believe how casual Joe was, considering that the authorities were just waiting for the opportunity to put him under the jail.

"Yeah. They can follow me all they want, though. My hands stay clean. I stay one step ahead of them mu'fuckas at all times." Joe fixed his cufflinks. "They couldn't catch me if they wanted to anyway."

Joe looked at the rearview mirror and locked eyes with his driver. He nodded slowly, signaling for his driver to speed up. He was ready to have a little fun with his tail.

The driver put the pedal to the floor, and the luxury vehicle weaved in and out of traffic at 100 miles per hour. The speed of the car was far too much for the Ford Taurus to keep up with, and within seconds, the FBI was MIA.

Joe pulled out a pre-rolled blunt and looked over at Malek. "See, I told you they can't fuck with me!" He lit the blunt and took a pull. Circles of smoke billowed from his mouth as he exhaled.

Malek grinned at how easy it was for them to shake the other car. "You a crazy mu'fucka."

They pulled onto the block that Joe had assigned to Tariq. The next thing Joe and Malek knew, the driver hit his brakes abruptly, causing the tires to screech. Within seconds, they noticed the skinny man who had jumped in the middle of the street in an attempt to flag down Joe's car.

"What the fuck?" Joe's eyes darted toward the front.

The driver immediately put the car in park and jumped out with his gun in palm. He rushed over to the man, grabbed him by the neck, and pressed the gun to his temple. "What the fuck is yo' problem? I should blow yo' brains out."

"Now hold up, youngblood. I just want to talk to Jamaica Joe for a second," the man stated nervously.

Joe looked closer as his henchman pinned the man down on the hood of the car. That's when he recognized the familiar face. "Oh, that ain't nobody but Scratch, that crazy-ass fiend," Joe said as he relaxed back on his seat. He knew Scratch from back in the day. Joe actually used to look up to Scratch in the '80s. Scratch used to be the dope man, but when he hit his own pack, he switched sides in the game. Instead of being the pusher, he became the user.

Figuring it was time to come to Scratch's rescue, Joe cracked his window a little bit and signaled for his henchmen to let Scratch come over to the car. "It's all good, man. Bring him over."

When the henchman released his grip, Scratch immediately rose up and massaged his neck. "Damn, youngblood, you didn't have to do Scratch like that," he said, talking about himself in third person, a habit that he always had.

Scratch walked over to the back door, and Joe rolled down his window, exposing his face.

"Scratch, you could've gotten yourself killed, fam," Joe told him.

"Ah, nah. You know it take a lot more than a car to kill good ol' Scratch." He smiled, displaying his rotted teeth—what he had left of them anyway. "Look, man, I got some valuable information for you, ya dig?" Scratch said, scratching his arms and neck.

"Some valuable information, huh?" Joe asked skeptically.

"That's right. You know I wouldn't come at you with no bullshit, Joe."

Joe thought for a minute and then nodded. "Get in."

In all of Joe's dealings with him, Scratch had never tried to play or run game, so if Scratch said he had some valuable information, then nine times out of ten, he did. All Joe had to do was determine just who the information was most valuable to.

Jamaica Joe and Malek slid over, making room for Scratch to sit down. As soon as Scratch entered the car, a foul stench filled their nostrils as the horrendous body odor punched them in the face.

Malek frowned his face and put his hand over his nose, trying to avoid the smell. "Damn, man," he said, waving his hand and then rolling his window down a bit. "I got some priceless information for your ass too—Soap and water works." Malek stuck his head out the window.

Jamaica Joe grew irritated at the odor and couldn't wait to rid himself of Scratch's presence, but he had to see what info the fiend had for him. He wasn't trying to make small talk with or smell Scratch for longer than he had to. "Yo, what you got to talk to me about, fam? Make it quick, 'cause you smell like death," he barked.

"Look, youngblood, Scratch was in the dope house, ya dig. And that cat, Tariq, was talking all greasy and stuff, saying he was the next big thang on the North Side and that you ain't gon' be the boss for much longer. He didn't notice Scratch, though. He was too busy talking. I heard everything he was saying. He said he was going to set you up to get you killed so that you'd be out of the way . . . and some other li'l nigga you been joined at the hip wit' these past days."

That last comment had gotten Malek's attention. He knew just what li'l nigga Tariq had been yapping about. He turned and faced Joe and Scratch.

An angry expression covered Joe's face. "What

the fuck you talkin' 'bout, Scratch?" Joe grabbed Scratch by his collar.

"I ain't say it," Scratch said, raising his hands in surrender. "Don't kill the messenger. Scratch just repeating what that nigga Tariq said. He gon' set you up, man."

The thought of someone setting him up instantly enraged Joe. Malek remained calm and silent as he watched the scenario unfold.

Scratch was shaking uncontrollably as his eyes shot wide open. "You know me, Joe. Scratch wouldn't lie to you, man. You know that. Scratch ain't never came to you wit' no bullshit. You know that, man. You know that, right?" Scratch swallowed hard as he tried to read the expression on Joe's face. Unable to, he decided to keep talking. "Tariq was saying something about setting you up with a fake buyer from Detroit and taking you out once you got there. Scratch is keeping it real, man. You've got to believe me, Joe," Scratch pleaded, talking so quickly that his words ran together.

Joe paused and thought about everything Scratch had said. Just earlier that week, Tariq had informed Joe that he had a potential buyer that was looking to cop heavy weight from him. He also said that it was a cat from Detroit, and mentioned that dude insisted that he wasn't gon' fuck with nobody but Joe in closing the deal.

"What is this nigga talking about?" Malek finally asked as he looked at Joe.

"I don't know, but I'm about to find out." Joe took out his cell phone and pushed the speed dial button for Tariq. The phone rang a couple of times before Tariq picked up.

"What's good, fam?" Tariq answered.

"Ain't nothin'," Joe said, trying his best to keep his cool until he got to the bottom of things. "Yo, about that trip this weekend, though, I can't make it. I'ma send one of the little niggas with you to watch your back, just in case some shit jump off. You know what I'm saying?"

There was a pause. Joe could hear Tariq take a deep breath, as if his brain was churning, trying to come up with his next words to say.

All Tariq knew was that he had to make the deal go down as planned. He had already lined up his soldiers that he was going to take with him to the top. What would he look like if his word wasn't bond? As far as he was concerned, Joe not coming through was not an option. He had to make it happen.

"Fam, I'm telling you, he ain't fucking with nobody else." Tariq used the most convincing tone he could muster. "He said he wants to deal directly through you. He a real paranoid mu'fucka, nah mean?" Tariq lied. "You know how it is when niggas be hatin'. He gotta watch his back, so he only wants to deal with the head, not some cat who might be trying to take his spot."

The irony of Tariq's words were killing Joe, but he maintained his composure. "Yeah, fam." Joe chuckled. "I know exactly what you mean. Nonetheless, I can't fuck with it. I got to shoot to Miami for the weekend on business."

"Joe, I really think this cat is a major player. He upped his order to fifty bricks, rather than thirty," Tariq said, thinking fast.

"Word?" Joe said, hearing the nervousness that

laced Tariq's voice. Hell, he was even starting to talk just as fast as Scratch, if not faster.

"For real. You gon' do it?" Tariq asked. "I mean, I can get at dude and let him know you got bigger business going on besides him and that y'all can reschedule the meeting, but I don't know, man. He might feel a little slighted and not want to fuck with you after that. And we talkin' about fifty bricks."

Joe grew a very suspicious look on his face and glanced over at Malek, who had been listening to the conversation intensely. Joe didn't want to believe that his man was setting him up, but he knew that the game didn't breed real niggas anymore, so anything was possible. Anybody could become an enemy, and his suspicions were now set on Tariq.

Malek whispered, "It's a setup, man. I can feel it."

Joe nodded his head in agreement, knowing that Tariq had tried to backdoor him.

"All right, I'll meet you at Atlas on Saturday morning," Joe stated just before he flipped down his cell phone. He shook his head in disbelief and then took a long pull of the blunt that he'd set in the ashtray earlier.

Joe then looked over to Scratch. "I guess you were telling the truth, man." He shook his head, still unable to grasp the fact that his man had turned on him. "Tariq ain't never asked me to go meet a buyer with him until now. He knew that I wouldn't let a fifty-brick sell bypass me either. Niggas playin' fo' keeps," Joe said, disappointment on his face.

Joe let out a deep sigh. "Get out." He leaned over Scratch and opened the door so that he could make his exit.

Scratch started to get out, but then hesitated. "Well, I was wondering, ya know, since I, uh," Scratch stammered, "looked out fo' you . . ." He swallowed hard then continued. "Why don't you, uh, you know, look out fo' Scratch?" He scratched his arms and avoided looking in Joe's eyes.

"I knew there was a catch." Joe reached into his pocket and pulled out a diamond-encrusted money clip shaped in the initial *J*. He peeled off two hundred-dollar bills and placed them in Scratch's lap.

Scratch's eyes lit up when he saw Benjamin Franklin's face. Just as quickly as Joe dropped the cash, Scratch scooped it up and slid out of the car. "Thanks, man. Scratch 'preciate it! Yeah, Scratch sho' 'preciate it."

They could hear him still shouting as they drove off.

Malek, finally able to inhale fresh air now that Scratch was gone, took a deep breath. "I knew Tariq was a bitch-made nigga. I knew it," Malek said as his mind began to spin.

A while back, during that shootout when those South Side niggas were trying to rob Joe, Malek had been only seconds away from blowing Tariq's brains out. And it had nothing to do with the fact that Tariq had set up the whole thing. As a matter of fact, to this day, Malek, like Joe, was none the wiser that Tariq was behind the whole shootout. Malek just wanted to shoot him as payback for what he had learned a few minutes prior to the shootout—what Tariq had done to his ex-girlfriend, Halleigh.

Out of respect for Joe, though, Malek fell back. He knew that Tariq had been Joe's right-hand man for some years, and he didn't want his beef with Tariq to fuck up business for Joe. Regardless of how tight or cool Malek and Joe were, Malek knew that things changed when one person fucked up the other's money.

Just when Malek was about to pull the trigger and blow Tariq's brains out, Joe had approached him. So, Malek shook it off, but he knew that Tariq's days were numbered. Now, with the information Scratch had given them, it was time for the countdown. Malek was sure Joe wouldn't mind at all if he took him out.

"So, what you thinkin', man?" Malek inquired as they pulled up in front of the dope house where Tariq was.

Joe shook his head as he stared out of the window at the house. "It's always the people who are closest to you that want to cross you." Joe slammed his hand down on the seat. "Fuck!" Joe gritted through his teeth. "Should kill that nigga."

"Yeah, and I wish I had took that mu'fucka out when—" Malek paused.

Joe was silent for a minute and then said, "Is that why, during that shootout, your aim was a little, how should I say, off?"

Malek looked at Joe in surprise. "You saw that?" Since Joe had never spoken on it, Malek hadn't been sure whether Joe was fully aware of his intentions with Tariq that day at the shootout.

Joe nodded. He could tell by the expression on

Malek's face that he was wondering why he hadn't said anything before now, so Joe put his mind to rest. "I didn't say anything because I figured your mind was all twisted. I mean, you had just run into your old girlfriend and shit, and I know how she be having a nigga's mind fucked up, so I let it go. Besides, I figured, if you had wanted that nigga dead, you would have handled yours right then and there. You had a perfect, clear shot."

Malek sighed. He was glad that Joe hadn't held that against him and placed him under the microscope of suspicion.

"But don't worry," Joe said as he puffed and exhaled, "this time I'm going to handle the situation. I got something for his ass." Joe reclined in his chair and signaled for his driver to pull off.

Chapter Three

Tasha pulled down the sun visor in her car to check her makeup in the mirror. She released a deep sigh before she flipped the visor back up. Butterflies had the nerve to be fluttering around in her stomach.

"Get it together," she told herself. "Since when have your skills failed you?"

Tasha was the queen of manipulation, which is one of the reasons why she had done her job of looking after the girls so successfully. Whatever Manolo hadn't been able to convince the girls of doing, she stepped in and made shit happen. Well, now, once again it was up to her to make shit happen, and, this time, lives were on the line.

Taking a deep breath, Tasha exited the car. As she walked into the Flint Police Department, a look of contempt crossed her face. She hated the police and everything associated with them, but desperate times called for desperate measures. Heads turned as the police officers admired her shapely legs, which stretched out beneath the red shirtlike dress she had ordered from a Frederick's of Hollywood catalog. It fit just tightly enough to reveal the outline of her round behind.

As Tasha walked by officers who were just standing around shooting the breeze or updating one another on police business, she noticed the lustful stares, and a smirk crossed her face. *Your pockets can't afford this pussy. Fuckin' pigs,* she thought while turning her nose up and making her way over to the front desk.

"What can I do for you?" an officer asked. He was reading the *Daily Journal* and barely even looked up to acknowledge Tasha.

"I'm here to see Detective Troy Davis," she responded.

Tasha figured that her visit to Officer Troy was long overdue. After all, he was the cop who Manolo supposedly had in his pocket. He was supposed to look out for them—more so look out for Manolo and his shady dealings. But if Tasha had her way, the tables were about to get turned fast enough to make Manolo a dizzy man. Besides, Tasha felt that, in a way, Officer Troy owed her, and it was payback time. After all, it was Tasha's pussy that had sealed the deal between him and Manolo. Her trick with Officer Troy had brought her out of years of retirement, so as far as she was concerned, it was time for him to pay the true piper.

"Have a seat. I'll see if I can track him down," the officer behind the desk responded to Tasha, reading one more line before putting the paper down and picking up the phone.

Tasha nodded and went and sat down. She

crossed her legs and massaged them suggestively as she waited for Officer Troy to come into sight. She had to make sure that he caught her getting her sexy on. She needed his help and knew that she would have to give a little to get a little. Tasha had to admit, not being conceited but convinced, that with her "work-'em" attitude, Officer Troy shouldn't be a problem. She knew that she looked good, and if the attitude didn't do the trick then, with her "fuck-'em" dress on, she was sure that Detective Troy Davis would take the bait.

"Miss Tasha."

She looked up to see none other than Officer Troy standing there, looking his usual lame, bald-head self.

Why couldn't he have at least laid off the doughnuts since the last time I saw him? Tasha thought, turned off by his protruding gut. *But fuck it. This is 'bout business.*

"Well, well, well," he chimed, "to what do I owe this unexpected surprise?" Troy rubbed his hands together and approached her, licking his lips as he looked her up and down. He knew firsthand that Tasha tasted as good as she looked.

This cornball-ass nigga. Tasha flicked her hair behind her shoulders. She did all she could to ignore the fact that Troy's bald head was shaped funny, that he'd had one doughnut too many, and, worst of all, that he was part of Flint PD—a stinkin' cop. But she needed something, so she'd have to put on her game face and play her hand right.

"Is there somewhere we can go to talk, you know, privately?" she asked, batting her eyes then allowing them to travel down to his crotch, which was only partially visible due to his bulging gut hanging over his belt.

"Yeah, let me show you to my office," he replied.

Tasha stood.

"After you." He held out his hand, allowing her to walk through the doorway first.

She walked with him through the precinct. When he put his hand on the small of her back and massaged it gently, she knew that she had him right where she needed him to be. Now she just had to go in for the kill.

They went into a small, messy office. He closed the door behind them, leaving on the other side a few drooling fellow officers who wished they could be in his shoes. He pulled out a chair for Tasha and then took a seat behind his desk.

"So . . . what can I do for you, Tasha? What is it that you want from me?" He leaned back in his chair and put his hands behind his head. He, too, had intentions of getting her right where he wanted her. It was an open playing field right about now, and anyone's game to win.

"Why does a girl have to want something?" she asked sweetly, giving him a genuine smile. Something about Officer Troy's tone let Tasha know that he wasn't as naïve as she'd assumed he was. She knew that she would have to play her cards right in order to get him to help her out.

"Because you haven't said one word to me since our little rendezvous at Wild Thangs. And that was, what, over a year ago?" He rocked back and forth in his office chair. "I even been up in there a few times. I figured since your boss owns the strip club, I'd maybe catch you in there. Guess I was wrong."

"Well, you know how it is in my line of work. A girl gets busy."

"Oh, but now all of a sudden your busy schedule has permitted you to just show up here out of the blue looking for me?"

Tasha shrugged as if to say, "That's what it looks like."

"Well, I got news for you—My luck ain't that fuckin' good, sweetheart. So let's try this again. What can I do for you?"

Tasha knew it was time to change her strategy. She didn't want to insult Troy any further by making him think she was taking him for a fool. She was confident, however, that by the end of the day he'd be playing the fool anyway.

She let her shoulders drop, and with a serious look on her face, she began her spiel. "Okay, I'm not gon' try to game you because I know you ain't falling for the bullshit anyway."

"You damn right about that, shorty, so let's just be real."

Tasha smiled because she had Troy thinking that he was in control. Using reverse psychology, she was still gaming his ass, making it seem like he had the upper hand. She had to give herself a pat on the back because she was truly one of a kind. There wasn't a man alive who could outsmart her. Not even Manolo, and she'd soon enough prove it.

Tasha wasn't like the other girls when it came to Manolo. He didn't have to trick or manipulate her into becoming a Manolo Mami. She knew exactly what she was getting into when she'd met South Side's most notorious pimp. Her entire goal was to become a kept woman, and if proving her loyalty to this man meant selling pussy for a couple of years, then so be it. Her initial plan was always to become the madam, the ruler over all of the other girls. It just so happened that her plan came to fruition a little sooner than she'd expected.

Unfortunately, it wasn't only Tasha's hard work and loyalty that placed her on the throne, but a horrible incident that she would never forget for as long as she lived. Being the strong-headed fighter that she was, she didn't let the brutal assault by one of her johns keep her down. Instead, after she recovered, she used the situation to her advantage and convinced Manolo not to put her back on the streets. And so he allowed her to be the madam of the house—the kept woman. Now, she didn't have to turn one trick for the rest of her life if she didn't want to.

When he'd made the decision, Manolo took into consideration Tasha's past loyalty. Besides, the madam of the house definitely had to be somebody with Tasha's personality, someone who the girls knew they couldn't run over, even with a Mack truck. So Manolo took her off the streets and gave her charge over the girls.

"Okay, I need a favor," Tasha just came out and said to Troy.

"So the plot thickens," he replied sarcastically.

She raised her eyebrows and looked at him like he was crazy. "Are you gon' let me finish?"

"I'm sorry, sexy. Go ahead. I mean, what else do I have to spend my time doing?" He spoke with sarcasm. "There are only a few hundred criminals I could be out there busting."

"Well, speaking of criminals . . . I need you to raid Manolo's club," Tasha said bluntly.

"What do you mean, you want me to raid his spot? For show or something?" Troy asked with a puzzled look on in his face.

Manolo had been allowing him a free supply of pussy from the Manolo Mamis in exchange for "overlooking certain things." So Troy couldn't imagine why else Tasha, whom he had known to be clearly on Manolo's team, would want him to raid Wild Thangs.

"No, not for show," Tasha corrected him. "For real." She moved in closer to Troy as if she were about to tell him something top secret. "He's got ten bricks and a little over fifty thousand dollars in a wall safe in his office." She bit her tongue and knew that it was because she was snitching. Under any other circumstance, she wouldn't even be caught in a police station, but she figured Manolo had this coming to him, having watched him manipulate the minds of young girls for years.

Tasha knew she played a role in the manipulation too, which was why she felt a responsibility to help Halleigh, and Mimi, too, get their lives back on track. This was the reason she was abandoning her principles, snitching to bring down Manolo. She couldn't take back the heartache, pain, and

even the death that some of the prostitutes had
suffered in the trick game, but she could at least
save others from it. If ever there was a time she
needed redemption in her life, it was now. She
hoped that her efforts wouldn't be in vain.

Troy sat up in his seat and looked Tasha directly
in the eyes. "This ain't news to me. I know what
goes on in that club. The thing is, Manolo laces my
pockets here and there, if you know what I mean.
Or have you forgot?" He winked at Tasha and
rubbed her thigh. "So I'm already getting my cut,"
he stated frankly, giving her one hard smack on
the leg and then turning his chair away to let her
know that he wasn't interested.

As far as Troy was concerned, Tasha hadn't
brought any better deal to the table than he was already getting with Manolo. In addition to free
pussy from the Manolo Mamis, Manolo himself
threw Troy some cash on the side.

"Believe me, that little bit of paper Manolo
throwing you ain't got shit on what's sitting inside
that safe." Tasha knew she had to butter up the
deal to make it just a tad more tasty so that Troy
would want to take a bite. "I figure we could split
the take fifty-fifty. That's twenty-five stacks each . . .
not to mention the potential profit from the
bricks." She looked Troy up and down. "That's
what, two years' salary for you?" Tasha stated, hoping to convince the crooked officer to see things
her way. Otherwise, she'd have to walk out of his
office with the risk of him ratting her out to
Manolo, and she knew what the end result for her
would be if he did.

Troy got a little curious and asked Tasha, "Why would you be telling me this? Manolo's pimpin' your pretty ass. I mean, no offense, but you Manolo's bitch. What do you have to gain?"

Tasha thought long and hard about the question Troy had just posed to her. She recalled the time when she first met Manolo. She was new in town and he put her on to a hustle. That, she couldn't deny. But that was before he was hard in the pimping game. At that time, he was pretty much just about getting money by any means necessary, not really finessing his business skills in the pimping game. And she was strong enough to deal with everything that came with the life. Some of the girls he'd turned out in the later years, however, were too weak to survive the game.

Halleigh's face popped into her mind. She knew that Halleigh was one of the weakest girls she'd ever had to deal with, and it was only a matter of time before she was found dead somewhere. The way Tasha saw it, she already had enough blood on her hands, and there wasn't room for more.

"My freedom," Tasha finally replied. "My freedom is what I have to gain." She stood from her chair and walked over to lock the office door.

Troy watched her every move. He turned his chair to face her as she closed the blinds and walked behind his desk. She lifted one knee to open his legs wide, her hands massaging the bulge growing in his groin.

"I'm chasing my freedom, Troy, and I'll do *anything* to get it," she whispered in his ear.

"Anything?" he whispered back, the lust making his voice seem deeper as he received the gentle massage in his private area.

"*Anything*," she replied.

He slipped a finger between her legs and smiled when he discovered that she wasn't wearing any panties. He had to admit, Tasha was a woman determined to get what she wanted.

Tasha's beauty had always enabled her to hustle men, and right now, Troy was merely another victim to be added to her long list of conquests.

Troy stood up and bent Tasha over his desk. Her voluptuous ass was calling for him. He began to grind against her as he undid his belt buckle.

Tasha played in her pussy, opening herself up for Troy and massaging her clitoris. She pulled a condom out of her bra and slid it to him. "Put the safety belt on it, daddy . . . and let's ride."

Troy, working with a good nine inches, rubbed his bare thickness against her vaginal walls. He wanted to feel just a touch of her rawness before slipping on the condom. "Put it on for me, baby," he ordered Tasha.

She turned around, took the condom package out of Troy's hand, then used her teeth to rip open the packet. She then stared Troy dead in the eyes as she teasingly slipped the condom on him. After making sure the condom was on just right, Tasha turned around and assumed the position. Troy played with Tasha's womanhood with the tip of his penis.

With Troy behind her, she didn't have to look at his face, and she was getting hot. She licked on her own nipples as she anticipated Troy's nine inches entering her.

He slid into her with ease and pumped her so hard that he caused her to crash against the desk. Items flew to the floor as she bucked against him, contracting her pussy on his shaft. He gripped her ass and opened and closed her cheeks as he rocked in and out of her. The sight of her slim waist, round behind, and the sound of her titties bouncing and making slapping sounds only excited him more. He began to moan in delight.

Tasha had to give it up to Troy. The nigga was fucking her right. If she had known that he was getting down like that, she might have given his ass some pussy the last time they'd connected at the strip club. Instead, Troy had left the club with Tasha's pussy juice on his face only. But, at the time, that was enough to make her feel disgusted by what she had to do. Prior to that night, Tasha had taken on her role as madam and stopped participating in any sexual acts with anybody, except for Manolo. So even though she was the one who ended up getting her rocks off with Troy's tongue action that night, a trick was a trick as far as she was concerned.

But now, Tasha was actually enjoying herself. She closed her eyes and bit her lip when Troy reached around and pinched her nipples. It turned her on, and before she knew it, she too was trying to silence her moans.

"Damn, this pussy so good," he whispered as his hips moved in circles, causing him to go even deeper inside of her. "Them other tricks ain't got nothing on your fine ass." Troy slapped her ass and stroked deeper.

"Mmmm, they learned from the best, Big Poppa," Tasha replied.

They were so loud that they had attracted a crowd outside of Troy's office. Someone knocked loudly, but Troy ignored it. They heard a voice from the other side.

"Everything all right?"

Still ignoring the interruption, Troy didn't respond. He just pulled out of Tasha, turned her toward him, then picked her up. He placed his stiff dick inside her again and pumped in and out of her while holding her in mid-air.

"Oh my God," she whispered in delight as he carried her around his office.

He reached his office door and pressed her against it as he continued to sex her.

"Damn, baby," Troy huffed and puffed.

He got so loud that Tasha had to put her hand over his mouth.

"I'm about to nut," he exclaimed.

"Nut for me, baby," she whispered, popping her pussy even harder, trying to get hers in too. She felt the gush between her legs as she came.

A few seconds later, Troy gripped her ass tightly as he experienced the best orgasm of his life.

After quickly releasing Tasha, he put his hand around his length and pumped every single ounce of cum out of himself and into the tip of the condom.

Tasha pulled her dress down and straightened it out. "So . . . do we have a deal?" she asked.

"Are you crazy? Hell yeah, we got a deal." He

breathed heavily, trying to catch his breath after that workout. "Whatever you want," he replied breathlessly as he began to clean himself up with some napkins he removed from around a paper cup of coffee.

Tasha, accustomed to getting her way, smiled. "Good. I need you to do it tonight."

"Tonight?" Troy questioned. "I need a little bit more time for that. I have to make sure I get the right men for the job, if you know what I'm saying. How about tomorrow night?"

"Tomorrow night will be too late," Tasha told him. "You know how the game is. Anything can change between now and tomorrow night. You need to make that hit tonight, or it might not even be worth it." Tasha walked up to Troy seductively. "And you know damn well it was worth it. Might even be worth a little somethin'-somethin' extra . . . if you know what I mean."

"Oh, I know what you mean all right, sweet thang." He looked Tasha up and down. "Tell you what—let me make a few calls. Now that I'm looking at things from another perspective"—He gave Tasha the once-over—"I think tonight is doable."

"Good." Tasha smiled. "I'm glad you took another look at things." She winked and then said, "So tonight, after you do your part, we'll split everything up sixty-forty, my favor."

Troy frowned as he pulled up his slacks. "Sixty-forty? What happened to fifty-fifty?"

"Well, Officer Troy, I, too, had to take another look at things. And, well, you know"—She looked down at herself—"this pussy ain't free." Tasha blew him a kiss as she sashayed away.

She opened the door to find a group of men standing there and eyeing her as if they were imagining what it would be like to be in Troy's shoes.

"Gentlemen," she greeted them, maneuvering between the men and exiting the building. She couldn't help the smile that spread across her face. She was about to gain her independence from Manolo. That was definitely something to smile about.

Tasha also knew that afterward, she, Halleigh, and Mimi would have to lay low. She decided that she would go back to her hometown of New York for a while until things cooled off. She thought about the bricks she would soon have on her hands to unload and turn into cash. That wasn't her forte, but she knew just who could help her do it. She was looking forward to the future now. After tonight, she hoped to be on the first flight out of Flint to New York. She couldn't wait to share the good news with Halleigh and Mimi as she made her way back to the house.

As Tasha drove, she thought momentarily about Manolo and what her betrayal would do to him. The more she thought about her relationship with him, the more she realized that Manolo had never done her wrong, not even once, since she'd known him. He'd always treated her like his main bitch, even before she ever officially was. As a matter of fact, it wasn't even his idea to put Tasha on the ho stroll in the first place; it was her own. She was paper-driven at the time, and whoring was just another way to add to the hustle.

Unlike the other girls, Tasha had been picky regarding who she would trick with. Not that the majority of the men were fine anyway, but there was a fine line between unattractive, plain ol' ugly, and completely disgusting. So if one of her johns would show up looking like he could make her throw up, Tasha would pass on the money, and not once did Manolo ever reprimand her for it. But if any other bitch had tried that, he would have been upside her head quick, fast and in a hurry.

Although Tasha had witnessed Manolo beat a couple of the girls senseless, he'd never laid a hand on her, except to embrace her or make love to her. Come to think of it, Manolo was the first man in Tasha's life who hadn't hurt her, and setting him up was how she was about to repay him.

All of a sudden, the sound of the tires rolling off the paved highway lane and onto the berm startled Tasha out of her thoughts. "Oh, shit!" she said as she regained control of the car and positioned the vehicle back in its lane. Now she just needed to get control of herself because there was no turning back at this point.

As Tasha continued driving, fond thoughts of Manolo were suppressed by visions of everything she had witnessed him doing to the other girls, especially Halleigh and Mimi. She recalled how Manolo had beaten Mimi almost unconscious one night at Wild Thangs, leaving her so bruised up that she couldn't put in work for almost a month. Then she recalled the time Manolo beat Halleigh when she refused to give him head as he had ordered her to do. And she didn't even want to think about the time he locked her down in the basement all those days.

Tasha couldn't help but shudder. How could

she have stood by all of these years and turn a blind eye? Guilt began to consume her.

Tasha realized that all the girls who had ever come through that house had taken one for the team by means of physical or mental abuse. Everyone but her. So, as she weighed her loyalty to Manolo against her sympathy for the girls, it was a no-brainer. She stepped on the gas and said, "Fuck you, Manolo. I'm out for self now."

Chapter Four

Tariq waited anxiously at Atlas Restaurant. Today was the day that he would become boss by default. He had spent the last few weeks mapping out his master plan, and now it was all about to go down. Tariq hadn't been shy about bragging of his efforts, before they were even played out, to any member of his team that had been willing to listen. But he felt comfortable bringing only one of his workers into the actual scheme.

Poppa, one of Tariq's workers, would wait for them to arrive at a rest stop halfway between Detroit and Flint. That was the spot where Tariq decided to take out both Joe and Malek, and Poppa was going to be the triggerman. Tariq was counting on Joe bringing Malek along. He knew that Malek already had a thing against him, and if Joe turned up dead on a run he had set up, Tariq knew that it wouldn't take long for Malek to put two and two together. Then a war would be on between the two of them. But by the same token, Tariq knew that Malek was like Joe's little shadow, and more likely than not, he would be tagging along.

The plan was one that couldn't fail, let Tariq tell it. After Poppa took out Joe and Malek, Tariq was going to leave their bodies there to rot, and take off with not only the bricks of cocaine, but with his newfound boss status. It was cut and dried. The only thing for him to do now was to wait.

After leaving the restaurant, Tariq sat out in the parking lot in his 2007 Suburban. That was the spot where he was supposed to meet up with Jamaica Joe and Malek. Any other time, he would have been bitter about the young buck rolling with them to handle grown folks' business, but this time, he was glad that Joe was bringing Malek along with them, so that he could kill two birds with one stone.

Tariq looked in his rearview mirror and saw his man in the rear hatch with a pistol gripped tightly. He looked straight ahead as he gave nineteen-year-old Poppa some last-minute instructions. "Yo, fam, you have to stay quiet, and don't do anything until I give you the signal."

"I got you, man," the young gun assured Tariq.

"Remember, when I pull into the rest area and turn the music up, bang them."

"Ain't they gon' think it strange when you pull over and shit?"

"I'm going to tell them I have to pull over to piss. That's when you do it, man." A half smile spread across Tariq's lips as he pictured the bloody scene. "Two shots to the head apiece. I got the body bags in the back. We gon' toss them into the river right by the rest stop. It's a perfect setup. All head shots, got it?"

"I got you, man," the boy hissed. "We went over this a million times already. If you doubted my skills, then you shouldn't have put a nigga on, ya heard." Poppa was lightweight offended. Tariq going over the plan with him repeatedly made it seem like Tariq thought he couldn't handle his business like the big boys. Poppa couldn't remember how many times he had told these cats that age ain't nothin' but a number. He was like Michael on *The Wire*. He could take out the best.

"Well, mu'fucka, I don't care how many times we have to go over this, li'l nigga. You got to hit they ass right, feel me? Any mistakes could cost you your life. Joe stay strapped, and I know Malek's ass is going to have his banger, so you just make sure you do the shit right. You gotta be quick. I don't want to have to pull out my piece and cover your ass," Tariq spat.

"Oh, nigga don't want to get his hands dirty, but wanna be the boss?" Poppa chuckled under his breath.

"What was that shit, man?" Tariq turned around and asked.

"Oh, nothing, man, I was just sayin', You the boss." Poppa smiled and then quickly erased it.

Tariq turned back around. That's when he saw Joe's car pull into the parking lot. He could feel his heartbeats increase, and the palms of his hands got a little sweaty. He wiped his hands down his pants and then calmed himself down, trying to look normal.

"It's showtime!" Tariq sang. "This is going to change both of our lives. We gon' be like Jerry Maguire and shit. We Tom Cruise and Cuba. I got some shit going on with Sweets, and we are all going to come together." Tariq told more of his full plan. "I'm going to run the North Side and make you my right-hand man, young gun. You ready to become a legend, nigga? This is where you earn yo' stripes."

Poppa got himself into a comfortable position in the back, where his marks wouldn't be able to see him. "I'm ready."

Malek drove Joe's Lexus coupe into Atlas Restaurant parking lot and noticed that Tariq's truck was parked toward the back. He then looked over at Joe, who was sitting next to him. "You sure you want to roll out with him, knowing that it's a setup?" Malek parked the car.

Joe said, "Do you trust me, Malek?"

"No doubt," Malek answered. "You my man."

"Roll with me on this one then, fam. I got this under control." Joe grabbed his pistol from his glove compartment and tucked it in his waist. He then gave Malek a look, as if giving him one last opportunity to break out.

Malek was skeptical and didn't know what Joe had planned, but he trusted him and was willing to have his back through whatever, especially if it meant seeing Tariq's head roll. Malek gave him a nod, letting Joe know that he was "ride or die."

As Joe and Malek got out of the vehicle, Malek's heart was pounding, not out of fear, but pure adrenaline. He didn't know what to expect, and he didn't see the logic behind Jamaica Joe walking into a setup. He guessed Joe didn't want to believe that his right-hand man would do him harm, and was hoping that he would have a change of heart and back out.

This nigga got balls, for real, Malek thought. *I'm keeping my hands on my banger at all times. That's my word.*

Joe instructed Malek to get the duffle bag from his back seat. Malek did as he was told, and then the two headed toward Tariq's truck. When Joe approached it, he opened the back passenger's side door.

"What up," Tariq said simply, looking over his shoulder at Joe.

"Handling this business," Joe replied. "That's what's up."

"Then let's ride out. Get in."

Joe hesitated for a minute. "I was thinking we ride out in my whip. You ain't really had a chance to roll in my new ride. Besides, I kinda wanna ride in the comfort of my own home, if you know what I'm saying."

Malek, who had one hand on the front passenger's door and the duffle bag in the other, paused to see what the deal was, whether they were going to ride in Tariq's vehicle or Joe's.

"Well, uh, you know I done, uh," Tariq started, with Joe trying to read the expression on his face and his body language, "I done got an oil change and shit and gassed up, you know."

Tariq, not wanting to look too suspicious, added, "But we can roll in your whip if you want to. It's all good." Tariq took his keys out of the ignition as if he were all gung ho about riding in Joe's car, but inside he was waiting for Joe to say the words that, within seconds, he eventually spoke.

"Nah," Joe said. "We can go on and take your shit. My shit almost on empty, and I ain't trying to make no stops riding dirty. You know what I mean?"

Breathing a silent sigh of relief, Tariq replied, "Yeah, I know what you saying."

Joe looked over at Malek and nodded for him to go ahead and climb in, which he did.

Malek and Joe hopped into Tariq's truck. Joe sat in the back, just like he always did. He never liked anyone to sit behind him. Malek sat up front with Tariq, who pulled off as soon as they were both in.

Tariq looked in the rearview mirror and addressed Joe. "What's good, fam?"

Joe nodded. "Like I said, just trying to make this money . . . *fam.*"

Joe, as hard as it was for him, maintained his composure toward this man who had for years called himself his right-hand man. Tariq had served as his confidant, his ace. Now it sickened him that he had to share the same air with him . . . but not for long. It was do or die. One of them was gon' do, and the other was gon' die. But which one?

Tariq looked at Malek and put his hand out to greet him. "What's good, Malek?"

Malek didn't even respond; he just kept his head straight.

Tariq's actions were a dead giveaway to Joe and Malek. Both Malek and Joe couldn't help but notice how out of character Tariq was acting already. Tariq never spoke to Malek. His jealousy of him had always been present, and he displayed it by being silent and giving Malek the cold shoulder. But today he made an exception. That didn't sit well. If Malek and Joe hadn't known something was up before now, Tariq's actions tipped them off for certain.

Malek watched Tariq pull his trembling hand back. *This nigga has got to be the dumbest mu'fucka in Flint. Look at this nigga.* It was obvious that Tariq's nerves were getting the better of him. It was written all over his face, and his uneasiness was evident.

Joe didn't want Tariq to sense that they knew something was going on, so he said, "Yo, fam, you sure this nigga is a hundred percent?"

"I'm sure. He is getting money out in the *D*. My uncle used to run with him back in the day. The nigga is one hundred percent, for sure. Square business!"

"If shit don't go down as expected, I'm holding you personally responsible, you feel me?" Joe told Tariq.

Tariq glared at Joe through the rearview mirror before saying, "Don't worry, boss. I promise that if things don't go as you expect them to, I'll be glad to take full responsibility." Tariq then turned his attention back to driving.

For the next thirty minutes, the three of them rode on I-75 without sound, everyone attending to their own thoughts. Poppa lay slumped in the back, trying to remain as quiet as possible. His heart raced a hundred miles per minute as he gripped his .45 automatic pistol. He was ready to go through with the plan. All he had to do was just wait for Tariq to pull over at the rest area so that he could earn his stripes.

Ever since he was twelve, when he did his first hit, Poppa felt like he always had something to prove in the streets. He was tired of people taking him for some okey-doke Negro. Although his history had just been poppin' off niggas for pay, which was how he came about the moniker *Poppa*, this wasn't no ordinary work for hire. He was caught up in a situation with the king of the North, which would earn him more street credit than he had ever imagined. Ready to make a real name for himself in the streets and shut niggas up from ever doubting his skills again, Poppa sat back and waited for his cue, which didn't take long to come.

"Yo, I got to piss like a mu'fucka." Tariq squirmed in his seat. "Here's a rest area coming up," he said as they passed the sign. "I'ma pull over real quick."

"Yo, you can't wait until we handle this business, fam?" Joe asked, hoping that Tariq would change his mind and not go through with it. "I said I didn't want to make no stops riding dirty. Fuck, we could have taken my car if we was gon' be stopping any damn way."

"I got to go now," Tariq said nonchalantly as he frantically kept checking the rearview mirror.

Once they came upon the ramp and Tariq exited the highway, the tension in the truck grew, as everyone knew something was about to go down.

Tariq pulled into the rest area and threw the car in park. He looked around and saw that no other cars were at the rest stop, and he knew this shit was destined to go down. Luck was on his side. Now he didn't have to worry about someone hearing the gunshots, or having to take out any extra heads. Hopefully Poppa would be quick about his business before any other cars pulled up.

"I'll be right back." Tariq turned up the music and yelled, "Y'all can just chill and listen to this new Scarface CD."

As Tariq got out of the car, Malek slowly slid his hand to his waist and waited for shit to pop off. He kept his eyes burned to Tariq's back. If his eyes could shoot bullets, Tariq would be full of holes the way Malek was glaring him down.

Tariq walked toward the men's restroom with a quick pace. He could hear his heart beating as he braced himself for the gunfire that he anticipated. He thought back to the time when he and Joe were as tight as blood brothers. He would have killed for Joe. As a matter of fact, he had killed for Joe on several occasions. Now the game had changed—well, at least the players were about to change anyhow. And Tariq knew that there was no turning back now. He could only stand in wait to hear the gunshot blast come from the car, so that he could get it over with.

Tariq might have talked a good game, and as big as his talk was, one might've thought his bullet game would be just as big.

Poppa had even asked him why he didn't save himself the money and the trouble and just pop Joe himself, but Tariq turned the tables on Poppa by asking him why he wanted to know. Was he scared to put in the work? Not one to back down from a test, Poppa ceased his questioning and accepted the job.

In truth, even though Tariq had popped off a couple of cats before, he just didn't have the heart to kill his man and Malek himself, so he was content with letting Poppa handle it. Poppa had no idea that Tariq was planning on slumping him after he killed Joe and Malek. Tariq didn't want any connections to the murder, so he had to get rid of all links that involved him. He had one mission and one mission only, and that was to take over. He didn't need no little young-ass sidekick, like Joe obviously thought he needed. Although he had admired Joe over the years, he didn't want to walk in his footsteps; he wanted to walk ahead of him, to take the game to a whole 'nother level of making money.

Tariq approached the bathroom, planning to come out an entirely different person. Just before he reached the door, he heard it.

Boom, boom! Two shots rang out from the car. Then two more. *Boom, boom!*

Tariq stopped in his tracks at the sound of the gunfire. He couldn't help but exhale as he turned around and rushed to the car, glad that it was all over with. The closer he got to the vehicle, the quicker his pace.

When he finally reached the car, he opened the driver's side door, and his heart skipped a beat with excitement. Funny how sometimes death could make a nigga's dick rise quicker than a butt-naked dimepiece sliding down a pole. Tariq couldn't hold back the smile when he saw Malek slumped on the dashboard. He looked back at Joe, who was hunched over in the seat. Tariq's smile grew even wider as he saw Poppa, who had a sinister grin on his face with the smoking gun in his hand, hovering over Joe.

"Hell, yeah! That's how you dead a nigga. We 'bout to take over!" Tariq yelled over the music before turning it off. "Ain't that right, my man?" he said to Poppa, giving the bodies another look.

But that was when Tariq had to do a double take because something wasn't right. Something was missing. The more Tariq observed the crime scene, he realized what was missing—blood. There was no blood on the scene. Not one single drop.

He immediately looked up at Poppa and began to back away, but before he could move, a smiling Malek had his gun pointed at Tariq's head.

Joe, without a scratch on him, slowly rose up, glaring into Tariq's eyes the entire time. "You look surprised, fam," he said. "Niggas was just catching some Z's while you went to take a piss." Joe chuckled, shrugging his shoulders. "What? You thought I was dead or something?" Joe leaned back in the seat, cool, calm, and collected. " 'Cause you look like you've just seen a ghost." He pulled out one of his pre-rolled blunts and lit it. He took a long drag and blew the smoke in Tariq's direction.

Malek, his pistol now pressed to Tariq's head, reached into Tariq's waist and relieved him of his strap. "You didn't even have the balls to kill me yourself," Malek said through clenched teeth. "You had to hire a gun? What kind of shit is that, *gangsta*?" Sarcasm laced Malek's words. "You had to go and hire Poppa?" Malek looked to Poppa while still talking to Tariq. "Unlike yourself, Poppa is loyal."

Tariq locked eyes with Poppa, who fired a look back at him that said, *"Nigga, what?"*

Poppa shrugged. A nigga had to do what a nigga had to do as far as he was concerned. But Poppa had to admit, when Tariq first presented him with the offer to put in work, he knew taking out someone with Jamaica Joe's status would give him major street rep. But it was also the type of rep that would come along with it, one of a traitor, that made him change his mind and tell Joe what Tariq was up to.

Poppa knew that Tariq was good for running his mouth. When all was said and done, knowing Tariq, he would have probably tried to take all the credit for taking Joe out, giving Poppa only minor props. But either way, Poppa knew what would come along with that, which was having the reputation of disloyal soldiers. Who would look up to them and want to put in work on their behalf then? As Poppa looked into Tariq's punk-ass eyes, he knew he'd made the right choice.

"You's a dumb mu'fucka," Joe told Tariq. "How you going to recruit one of my soldiers to hit me? Huh?" Joe chuckled. "I mean, he may be on your team, but the li'l nigga know where his pay come from. Did you really thing he was gonna bite the hand that feeds him?"

Tariq remained silent. He just kept staring at Poppa, not believing that he had double-crossed him, which was ironic, because that's the same thing Joe was thinking about Tariq.

"What the fuck you looking at, nigga?" Poppa finally spoke to Tariq. "Joe been letting me eat since I was sixteen. I'm a real nigga. I stay loyal. I saw what you were up to." Poppa pulled out the body bags that Tariq had placed in the back with him. "You brought three body bags with your stupid ass. What, you think just 'cause I ain't graduate, a nigga can't count? I knew what you was gon' do, bitch. Who the third bag for?" Poppa gripped his gun tighter.

"Fall back, man. I got it," Joe said as he looked over at a Lexus pulling up beside him.

Tariq heard company coming, and for a split second he was relieved. It might be an opportune time for him to get away. Surely Joe wouldn't do him in front of witnesses if he didn't have to.

Unfortunately for Tariq, the person in the car was no witness. It was one of Joe's henchmen, there to pick them up just in case Joe and Malek found themselves in a shootout or something.

Malek pressed the gun even harder into Tariq's head. The time was near, and he was itching to pull the trigger. He had long wanted to take out this punk-ass nigga anyway. Even before he found out that Tariq was one of the men who had raped Halleigh, the event that caused her to run away from home and fuck up her life in dealing with that cat Manolo in the first place, he had a bad feeling about Tariq. Something just wasn't kosher about him. But now it was on. He was just waiting on the word from Joe to pop off this coward.

Joe looked over to Malek. "It's time."

Malek smiled and cocked his piece.

"Look, Joe," Tariq spoke up, swallowing hard,

"how can you blame me? You didn't let me grow. You let Malek come in and you gave him the block I wanted. The block I had earned after all I've done for you."

"After all you've done for me, nigga?" Joe sat up and snapped, spit flying out of his mouth with every word. "You ain't did shit for me, nigga. You the one that had to eat. I just kept the mu'fuckin' cupboards full. But don't think for once you ever prepared my plate, nigga. Joe was gon' eat with or without you." Joe looked to Malek. "As you can see, and not that I like to quote bitches and shit"— Joe leaned back and pulled on his blunt—"but you ain't irreplaceable."

"But I was supposed to be yo' right-hand man, not him! Me!" Tariq shot back. "You let this nigga come in and take my spot!" The veins showed in Tariq's forehead, and tears formed in his eyes as he verbalized his jealous thoughts to Joe.

But Joe was unmoved. "Are you done, nigga?" he asked, nonchalantly puffing away.

Tariq braced himself and took a deep breath, knowing his life was about to come to an end. He stuck his chin up bravely and answered, "Yeah, I'm done."

Just before a single shot rang out, Joe said, "Good night."

Boom!

Malek put a bullet through Tariq's temple, and the driver's window suddenly looked like it had red tint. Tariq's upper body lay across the front seat, while his legs dangled outside of the truck.

It was Malek's first time catching a body. He didn't

know how it was going to make him feel after the fact, but it wasn't as bad as he had imagined. He had often wondered how dudes could just take another man's life and keep it moving day to day like it wasn't nothing. Now he knew. Taking Tariq's life was personal. He didn't do what he'd just done for himself; he did it for Halleigh.

"See you in hell, bitch-ass nigga," Malek spat. Then he put his gun back down in his waist.

"Clean him up, Poppa. Put him in one of them bags so we can toss him." Joe stepped out the car and casually walked to the ledge over the river. He stared at the water and continued to smoke as he thought about the turn of events that had just played out. He put his head down and shook it in disbelief. He never thought that Tariq would turn on him. In a matter of time, though, Joe knew he'd shake it off and keep things moving just as before. In spite of how tight and loyal he felt Tariq was, he also understood that backstabbing, murder, and lies were all a part of the drug game. It just hurt him that after all this time, Tariq was the one who had betrayed him.

"Keep yo' friends close, but your enemies closer," Joe whispered to himself as he tossed the blunt into the water. He looked back and saw Malek and Poppa carrying the black body bag with Tariq's corpse toward him so that they could throw it into the water.

Once they reached the ledge, they lifted and propped the bag full of dead weight, literally, onto the edge, preparing to push him over.

Boom! Joe put a bullet through Poppa's head,

causing him to fall over the ledge and crash into the water.

Malek jumped, dropping the bottom portion of Tariq's corpse.

"Damn, Joe! What you do that for?" Malek asked. "You at least could have warned me."

"I had to take him out," Joe admitted. "I would have always wondered, if I hadn't found out about the setup, would he have gone through with it? Just what move might that little nigga have made in the end if he hadn't counted three body bags?"

Prior to rolling to Detroit, Joe had managed to catch up with Scratch again and ask him to describe the worker that Tariq had been boasting to about his intent to set him up. When Scratch described the young cat Tariq had been talking to at the crackhouse, Joe knew it was Poppa. And it didn't take a brain surgeon to figure out that if Tariq was running off at the mouth to Poppa, he was going to try to recruit him to help. In spite of the fact that Tariq had always come through for Joe on any assignment he had ever given him, he knew that Tariq was smart enough not to try to pull this one off alone. And the fact that Poppa didn't come to him never sat well with Joe . . . and it never would have.

Malek remained silent and tried to stop his heart from beating so fast. He tried to conceal his nervousness, but Joe noticed.

"Let's get the fuck out of here," Joe said as he helped Malek push Tariq's body over the ledge.

Malek didn't realize it, but he had just moved up in the ranks by default. He showed Jamaica Joe a lot of loyalty and heart in that situation, and Jamaica Joe took note. Malek and Jamaica Joe jumped in the truck, with Joe's henchman following behind, headed back to Flint, two snakes lighter.

Chapter Five

Mimi was on stage working the pole as she looked out into the crowd. As always, Wild Thangs was packed, and dollar bills were scattered all over the stage during Mimi's show. Mimi didn't dance at the club on a regular, so it was always a treat for the regular patrons when she did. Manolo knew it meant extra incoming funds when a feature was in the house; and Mimi was indeed a feature.

She was always sure to call up all of her regular customers and let them know when she was going to be taking the stage so that they could be there to spread the love in the form of dollar bills and at least a twenty-dollar drink, but she was known to have dudes buy her hundred dollar drinks. Mimi had taken the liberty to insist that all her johns be in the house tonight for what she knew was her finale. And the idea of extra pocket change didn't hurt either.

As Keith Sweat's song "Chocolate Girl" played, Mimi put on the show of her life, sliding down the pole upside down spread eagle. She slowly straightened her legs and kicked them down, rising into a standing position as she looked out at the clapping crowd of men who had enjoyed her little stunt. She watched as they marched by the stage like an army of ants, dropping dollars. She even allowed a couple to stick some down her camisole, allowing them to get a quick free feel of her breasts.

A satisfying smile spread across her face as she looked out and spotted Manolo, who hadn't really been paying her a bit of mind. He was sitting in his VIP booth with Tasha, Halleigh, and his young killers, the Shottah Boyz.

Manolo was poppin' bottles as if he was the king of the city, and Mimi could tell that he was feeling himself. According to the plan Tasha had shared with her and Halleigh earlier, his night was going to go downhill from there on out, and Mimi reveled in the thought. She couldn't wait to see his downfall. After all the bad karma Manolo had put out into the world, he was finally about to get his.

Mimi reached high on the pole and gripped it with her hands. She wrapped her ankles around it, released her hands, and allowed her body to hang upside down once again. She then slowly slid down. This time, her little trick caught Manolo's attention. He loved when she did that move. She winked at him as she made her way down to the bottom of the pole.

Nigga, you better enjoy this night. It's gon' be your last free night for a while, Mimi thought as she reached her hands back up to grab the pole before her head touched the ground. Then she put her pussy in a customer's face and did a slow grind.

The man stuck out his tongue and licked her slowly. He had full access to her because of the crotchless camisole she was wearing, and the crowd went crazy when they saw the man feasting on her.

Mimi wasn't embarrassed or ashamed by her performance; she was all about her paper and was willing to do whatever it took to get it. She'd made a name for herself as one of the best dancers in Michigan, and she wanted to give her loyal fans a good finale and fill her Crown Royale bag at the same time. She knew that tonight would be her last time stripping on anybody's pole. She was done with the entire ho business and was ready to get money in a new way. She couldn't promise herself that it would be in a legit way, but she'd put her best foot forward.

After her set, Mimi joined Manolo at his table. He was drunk and feeling good when she sat down beside him. "Hey, Daddy," she greeted as she grabbed a drink from his hand and took a sip.

"What up? You got my cut?" he asked, referring to his percentage of her night's earnings.

His comment pissed off Mimi. He always tried to pull his pimp card when he was around his niggas. But she concealed her attitude as she reached into her camisole, pulled out her money, and handed it over to him. Since he had only been half paying attention to her, she knew that he missed a couple of times several men had given her cash. Ordinarily she would have held out on Manolo just a little bit, but she figured at this point in the game, she would choose her battles wisely. Besides, this fight would be over soon anyway. Tasha had told her that she would split her sixty percent from the safe with Mimi and Halleigh so that they would at least have something to get them started once they were no longer working for him. So Mimi wasn't tripping over the money she had just turned over to Manolo.

Mimi looked over at Halleigh and Tasha, who were sitting next to Manolo, one on each side of him. Mimi observed their smug expressions. She could tell that they were feeling the same way she was—thick. They finally had the upper hand on Manolo, and he was so stuck on himself, he didn't even realize it.

Everybody was loose in the club, and Manolo was talking big as usual. They partied for a couple more hours, and by midnight, the club was popping off proper.

Tasha checked her watch and knew what time it was. She scanned her surroundings discreetly. If everything went according to plan, Troy and his boys in blue would be there any minute.

Just like clockwork, less than five minutes later, the club was flooded with uniformed police officers. They stormed into the club with their weapons drawn. A couple of screams erupted throughout, but very few people were scared. It was typical for the po-po to raid the local strip clubs, be it legit or a shakedown. That's just how the Flint PD got down. Everyone put up their hands and watched curiously to see how the scenario was going to play out.

"Everybody on the ground! Now!" Troy screamed as he made his way to the VIP section, his fellow officers following right behind him.

Manolo was enraged. He didn't know what was going on. All he knew was that Troy should have given him a heads-up that boys in blue would be riding through. That way he could have made sure the place was clean—especially if Flint PD was sending dirty cops.

I'm paying this mu'fucka to turn his head to my business and he coming in here on some bullshit? He stood to his feet. "Fuck is going on, man?" he spat as Troy approached. "Thought we had a deal!"

Troy grabbed Manolo's arm and twisted him around, forcing him to lean over the table.

The Shottah Boyz reached for their pistols, but decided against it. They knew better than to catch a case by trying to come to Manolo's defense.

Troy applied the bracelets to Manolo's wrists and then pulled a search warrant from his back pocket.

"Fuck is you doing coming up in here? Fuck you looking for?" Manolo yelled.

As the police squad spread throughout the club, Troy commanded, "Turn this place inside out."

Troy wanted to make it look good, so he didn't go to the safe right away. He searched the club for about twenty minutes before he discovered the safe that, of course, Tasha had already informed him of.

"Jackpot, boys!" Troy announced. "Let's take him in to be processed." He placed the bricks in a duffle bag along with the money and then headed out of the club.

Tasha looked at Halleigh and Mimi. The satisfaction on their faces was priceless, but now it was time for her to go collect their money. "Stay here and clear out the club. I'm going to get our cut now before Officer Troy gets any ideas. I'll come back in about an hour," she stated before leaving the club.

Tasha drove toward Miller Road and parked her car in the empty shopping center lot. Just as planned, Troy was waiting for her. She eagerly hopped out of the car.

"I got to take ten thousand and two kilos of cocaine back to the station so that I can log it in as evidence," he informed her as she approached.

"What? You didn't tell me that."

"Look, my ass is the one who has to build this case against Manolo for him to do jail time. There's twenty thousand in there for you. You can also keep the rest of the dope. I can't do anything with that."

Tasha's eyes lit up when he said that. She knew that the eight bricks were as good as gold, so she shut up and accepted the deal. "Nice doing business with you, Troy," she stated with a wink.

"Very nice." Troy licked his lips and eyed her up and down. "Let me know if you'd like to do *it* again."

Tasha smirked. The sex was good, but it wasn't that damn good. She still hated cops, and she knew that she wouldn't make it a habit of dealing with him. She hopped back into her vehicle and pulled away.

When she arrived back at the club, Mimi and Halleigh were waiting patiently for her. She was surprised that they had gotten rid of everyone so quickly.

"You get the money?" Mimi asked, the dollar signs practically forming in her eyes.

"Yeah, I got it. There are twenty stacks here and eight bricks," Tasha replied.

"What are we gon' do with some dope?" Halleigh asked.

"Don't worry about it. I'm gon' holla at my brother. He lives in New York. We're going to visit him there. We'll let things cool down before we come back . . . if we come back."

Tasha divided the cash by giving herself $8,000 and then giving Halleigh and Mimi $6,000 apiece. She figured she should get a little more for putting the plan together and fucking with Troy to carry it out. Mimi and Halleigh had no objections.

"Look, y'all, no one can know that we set up Manolo's arrest, so we just have to keep our mouths shut and let things die down. Then I promise you that everything will be fine," Tasha said.

Halleigh smiled and hugged Tasha tightly. "Thank you, Tash. Thank you so much."

Mimi was busy flicking through her money when she burst out laughing.

Halleigh frowned. "What's so funny?"

Mimi shook her head and giggled some more. "Did y'all see Manolo's face when the police blew up his spot?"

Halleigh and Tasha joined in on the laughter.

Mimi shook her head. "His ass was getting ready to cry when they put those handcuffs on him."

"What goes around comes around," Halleigh stated. "I hope he rots in the mu'fucka."

"Let's get out of here." Tasha rose from her seat. "We've got a long drive ahead of us." Tasha had changed her plans to fly to New York, when she decided that she would take Mimi and Tasha with her. Leaving them in Flint was too risky. If they were with her, they couldn't talk.

The girls exited the club with a burden lifted from their hearts. Manolo had taken advantage of each of them in their own way. As they pulled away from the club, they felt safe and secure, knowing that their betrayal would be a secret that would never leave those four walls.

Just as Tasha, Halleigh, and Mimi drove away, Keesha came walking out of the club with envy in her eyes. She'd just overheard the conversation and knew it had to be worth something. She just had to figure out how she would use it to her advantage.

Chapter Six

"**O**h my God, can we stop and grab something to eat?" Mimi attempted to shift to a more comfortable position in the small car. "We've been driving for eight hours straight."

"We're almost there." Tasha looked at her watch. It was three in the afternoon. "We got like two hours to go. We've got all this shit in the trunk, so we got to keep it pushing until we unload the bricks. My brother will know what to do." Tasha had told the girls before they headed out that they were doing the thing in one straight shot, so if anybody had to eat or piss, they best do it before they hit the highway.

"I just want to get out of these clothes and take a shower," Halleigh added. "Does your brother even know we're coming?"

"No, I didn't tell him," Tasha confessed, "but it's not gon' be a problem. I haven't failed you girls yet, so just trust me."

* * *

The girls drove for three more hours before they finally arrived in Brooklyn, New York. They pulled up to a modest two-story home, and Tasha smiled when she thought of the familiarity she felt just being there.

"Let's go, bitches!" Tasha yelled excitedly at the thought of seeing her brother.

Halleigh and Mimi got out of the car and followed her up the walkway that led to the house. Tasha knocked lightly on the door and stood impatiently as they waited for an answer.

"I don't think he's here," Halleigh stated with a sigh as she leaned against the porch ledge.

"It doesn't matter. This dumb boy always keeps a key underneath his doormat." Tasha knelt down and lifted the mat. Just as she had predicted, her brother hadn't changed.

Leaving the key under the mat was a habit Tasha's grandmother had always had. That way if any of her children ever needed to come, they would always have a way in. That tradition had passed down to their mother as well. Even though Tasha's brother didn't have any children, he had picked up the habit too. Now Tasha could see why it was such a good habit after all as she scooped up the key and let herself into his home.

They entered the home and were greeted by a ten-foot foyer with a shiny hardwood floor.

"Damn, he's living nice," Mimi stated as she nosily walked around the house. It wasn't anything extravagant, but it was definitely better than what she had grown accustomed to. He was hood rich, with flat-screen televisions and nice leather furniture. A huge fish tank with exotic fish took up an entire wall. Surprisingly, the house was clean, but you could tell that it was a bachelor's spot.

Halleigh, too, was impressed with the sense of style as she looked around the four-bedroom home decorated in brown earth tones.

"Make yourselves at home." Tasha walked down the hallway and into one of the rooms. "I'm crashing in here. Y'all can pick whatever room you want," she said as she went inside and closed the door.

"How this bitch gon' tell us to make ourselves at home and this ain't even her shit?" Mimi stated with a laugh.

Halleigh ignored Mimi's comment. "I'm going to lie down before I pass out," Halleigh stated wearily. "That shower can wait. I can't even stand up long enough to wash up anyway."

Halleigh looked inside the remaining three rooms and chose the one that didn't look occupied, assuming that it wasn't Tasha's brother's. She pulled her shirt over her head, took off her jeans, and released her hair from the tight ponytail, allowing it to fall freely to her shoulders. She was tired, and all she wanted to do was sleep. She needed to wrap her mind around the fact that she no longer belonged to Manolo. She was free, the owner of her body again. Although she could never take back the fact that she'd lain down with more men than she could count in the name of money and security, she could take back what was hers, and that was peace of mind.

Her body had been abused and misused for so long that she no longer viewed herself as a lady.

She felt like a ho, and it would take a while for her learn to love herself again. But this was a start. The last two years of her life had been hell. She'd done things she never thought she would do, and had been through tribulations she thought would be the death of her. Now all she wanted to do was move forward.

Serenity took over her body, and as soon as her head hit the pillow, she drifted off into the deepest sleep ever.

Halleigh awoke and hopped out of bed. Her head was still cloudy, but she was grateful for the couple hours of peace that she had experienced while she slept. A note rested on the pillow beside her. She picked it up and read it.

Hal,

Mimi and I are going out to grab something to eat. We'll be back in a few. If you need anything, just call my cell. Your lazy ass probably won't even get up before we get back, but just in case, you know how to reach me. Oh yeah, make sure you get dressed. We're going out tonight to celebrate our new freedom.

Tash

"Damn! They could've woke me up. I'm starving," Halleigh crumpled the letter and tossed it aside. "And how am I supposed to get dressed when my bags are in her car?" She walked into the attached bathroom, quickly shed herself of her bra and panties, then stepped into the freestanding shower. She turned the handles and closed her eyes as the hot water streamed down on her. It felt so good against her skin, like she was washing all of her sins away.

All of a sudden the shower curtain was snatched back. Halleigh screamed in alarm as she tried to cover her naked body.

"Fuck is you?" a dude asked her.

"Do you fuckin' mind?" Halleigh screamed as she stepped out of the shower and searched for something to cover herself. "Get out!"

"This is my crib!" the dude responded. His eyes looked her up and down as a sexy smile crossed his lips. He reached over to his linen closet and grabbed a towel. "Here, cover yourself up, shorty."

She snatched the towel from his hands and wrapped it tightly around her body. Her hands were shaking, and he noticed how uncomfortable his presence made her.

"Now do you want to tell me who the hell you are and what you're doing in my house?" He made sure to calm down his tone because he could see that he'd frightened her. He followed her out of the bathroom and into his bedroom. He noticed that his bedsheets were wrinkled and looked back at her as he awaited an answer.

"I'm your sister's friend," Halleigh explained. "Tasha went out to get something to eat. I was sleeping, so she left without me."

The dude frowned his face and nodded his head. "Okay, let's call her," he said, not believing a word she'd said. He pulled a BlackBerry off his waist and flipped through it until he found his sister's number.

"Yo, Tasha, what's good, baby girl?" he asked when Tasha answered the phone. "Where you at?"

Dripping wet, Halleigh stood with her arms folded across her chest, the cold draft making her nipples stand at attention.

"I'm around your way, big bro," Tasha replied. "Me and my girls came into town earlier. You weren't home, so we let ourselves in."

"Yeah, I see," he replied. His eyes scanned Halleigh's physique, and she rolled her eyes. "You could've at least called me to let me know y'all were in my spot. You know how I get down. What if I had something up in here I didn't want y'all to see?"

"Boy, please . . . you leave a damn key under your mat. Anybody in the city can see what you got. Besides, it ain't too much we haven't seen already. I'm shopping down on Canal Street. I'll be back in a couple hours," she replied.

Halleigh sighed loudly. "Can you please tell Tasha that my clothes and stuff are in her trunk?"

Tasha's brother ignored Halleigh's request and said, "All right, sis, I'll holla at you when you get here." He disconnected the call and then said, "What's your name, ma?"

"Halleigh."

"I'm Maury," he said, walking over to his dresser. He opened a drawer and pulled out a white Prada button-up. He tossed it on the bed. "You can put that on until Tasha gets back with your gear. I'll be in the kitchen."

"Thanks." Halleigh followed him to the bedroom door and closed it as he walked out. "I'm-a kick Tasha's ass for leaving me up in here by myself," she mumbled, putting on the shirt and buttoning it up. The material swallowed her tiny frame, and she rolled the sleeves up before she walked out of the room. She found Maury sitting in the living room, waiting for her. She stood in the doorway.

He looked up when he felt her presence behind him. "Make yourself comfortable. I ain't gon' bite you, ma." He patted the seat beside him. "Then again, looks like you didn't need me to tell you to make yourself comfortable at all, now did you?"

Halleigh rolled her eyes and took the seat next to him.

He smirked at how timid she seemed to be. "I don't know why you acting all shy now. You already slept in a nigga's bed and everything," he joked.

A smile graced her lips. "I didn't know that was your room. I wasn't trying to be all up in your space."

"I'm not complaining. A beautiful woman waiting at home for me ain't exactly what I would call a bad thing," he stated, admiring her lovely features.

Halleigh felt his imposing stare and pulled her legs in, tucking them underneath the oversized shirt. "Now here you go," she stated in exasperation. She could smell Maury's game from a mile away. His compliments came out as if they had been used a million times before.

"What? I'm not lying, ma," he stated, a mischievous grin on his face.

"Whatever." Halleigh stood because she didn't want to be so close to Maury. Men made her wary, and being alone in the house with someone she barely knew didn't sit too well with her. She didn't know what it was like to be at ease around a man. The only person she'd ever trusted was Malek, and he left her high and dry at a time when she needed him most.

"Did Tasha say when she'd be back? I'm not trying to put you out or nothing," she said.

Maury smiled. He could see that he made Halleigh nervous. "Why are you nervous?" he asked.

Halleigh frowned. "I'm not. I just don't like the fact that Tasha left me up in here knowing that I don't know you. I don't trust everybody, so this is kind of awkward for me."

"You can trust me, ma. I ain't gon' kidnap you or nothing." Maury stood up and grabbed her hand, pulling her into the kitchen. "You ate?"

She shook her head and allowed him to lead her to a barstool that sat in front of the kitchen island. She sat down and watched him walk over to the refrigerator. She had to admit that Maury was fine. His baggy jeans and thuggish swagger made him sexy. He wore a red fitted hat, baggy jeans, and a black Sean John hoodie. Halleigh's eyes followed his every move as he stood with one hand on his belt buckle.

He looked back at her and turned his mouth up in a half smile when he caught her staring. "What you want to eat, ma?" he asked.

"Whatever you have is fine." Halleigh tried to hide the fact that she was blushing.

Maury frowned as he stared into the refrigerator. "Let's see, I got old lettuce." He pulled out a brown head of lettuce and set it on the counter. "I got some Gatorade, some eggs, but I don't know how long these been in here."

"That's okay. I'm not that hungry after all," she stated, laughter in her voice.

"You want to go out and grab something?" he asked.

"I don't have any clothes to put on, thanks to your sister."

"Okay then, let's see." He rubbed his hands together and thought for a moment. "You eat Chinese?"

Halleigh nodded.

"We can have them deliver it, and I'll put in a movie," he offered.

"Yeah, that sounds good."

Maury retrieved a Chinese restaurant menu he had hanging on his refrigerator. After asking Halleigh what she liked, he placed an order for their food.

When the food arrived, Maury grabbed a blanket and two pillows from the closet, and they sat on the floor watching movies and stuffing their faces. He noticed that Halleigh didn't say much, but she seemed to loosen up a little bit as they sat in each other's presence. They laughed at Martin Lawrence's *Runteldat*, and they seemed to be enjoying each other's company.

Before Maury knew it, it was almost midnight and Halleigh was asleep next to him. He picked her up, and as if she belonged in his arms, she rested her head on his chest as he carried her to his room. He didn't know why he didn't put her in one of the guest rooms. She just looked right in his bed, and since that was the room she'd chosen to sleep in earlier, he figured it was where she was most comfortable. After laying her down, he went back to the living room, plopped down on his couch, and finished watching the movies until he too went to sleep.

Chapter Seven

Malek walked into his small apartment in Grand Blanc, a suburb just outside of Flint. He went straight to the back bedroom, where his safe was located. He emptied the contents of a brown paper bag into the safe. He'd just made a pick-up from the money spot. He placed the two stacks neatly on top of the others and stared at the stacks of money he'd accumulated working under Jamaica Joe. He would hit Joe off with his take at the end of the week, but nevertheless, he was still getting money. His life had changed so quickly over the past couple of years. He once was a role model in the community, but now he was a certified D-boy and running blocks.

Malek began to think about Halleigh and how much he missed her voice, her presence, her touch. He couldn't believe that she fell into the lifestyle she had chosen. *I miss that girl so much. I can't believe she's out there trickin', though. That's not Halleigh. It's not her.* He walked into the living room and flopped down on his sectional sofa.

The last time he'd seen Halleigh, in the restaurant moments before they had the shootout with Sweets' crew, she had nothing but hate for him. Seeing him with Tariq, the man who had raped her, she wasn't trying to hear anything Malek had to say. Halleigh should have known him better than to think that he would knowingly team up with someone who had hurt her.

He thought about her constantly, but knew that the streets had a tight hold on her. Before Malek could even finish his thought, he heard a knock at his door. From the pattern of the knock, he instantly knew who it was. Also, he'd only let one person know where he lived, so he had a pretty good idea who was knocking. He got up to answer it, and when he opened the door, Joe was standing on the other side.

"What's good?" Malek slapped hands with Joe and walked into the back room to get Joe's cut. He'd planned to wait until the end of the week to break him off, but since he was there, might as well handle it now.

"What's going on, fam?" Joe asked as he walked in, closing the door behind him. He walked over to Malek's couch and took a seat. He looked around and chuckled. "Yo, you need to move into a bigger place. You getting money now. You gotta start enjoying it."

Malek, unlike other hustlers who were making paper, preferred to live modestly. What the hell did he need all that bling-bling for anyway? As far as he was concerned, all that flashy stuff did anyway was bring attention to him, which meant drama and trouble would soon follow. So he decided that he would stay low-key in the game. He'd seen enough black people get the things they wanted, yet end up begging for the things they needed. He wasn't going to fall into that trap.

Joe began setting up the chessboard that sat on Malek's coffee table.

A few minutes later, Malek emerged from the back room with a small duffle bag full of money, approximately $52,000. When he saw that Joe had set up the board, he immediately knew that Joe wanted to discuss something with him. Joe always played chess when he was telling Malek something important. Malek placed the bag by Joe's feet and took a seat.

Joe stared at the board, deep in thought, contemplating his first move. He knew that this move ultimately laid the foundation for the last. "I've watched you become a man in such a short period of time. I think you're ready to step into the big leagues, fam." Joe moved his pawn up on the board.

"What you mean?" Malek asked, his eyes on the board, contemplating his first move as well.

"After the shit that went down with Tariq, and with the feds being on me and all"—Joe paused, observing the board—"I need to fall back for a minute. I need to get out of town to clear my head, ya know?"

Malek replied with a simple nod.

"With that said, I want to give you the opportunity of a lifetime." Joe made his move.

Malek's full attention was on Joe, not even realizing that it was his turn to make a move.

Jamaica Joe pulled out one of his pre-rolled

blunts and lit it. He took a puff, exhaled as smoke rings rose above his head and then added, "I want to introduce you to my coke connect. I need someone to run the empire while I'm away, and you the only person I trust."

"Are you serious?" Malek knew that Joe was offering him a "key to the city," and he couldn't believe his ears. This kind of opportunity was every hustler's dream. He was offering him on a silver platter what Tariq tried to take. A smile covered Malek's face.

"I know you one hundred. I can't say that about most of the niggas in my circle. Tariq was proof that you can't trust niggas, feel me?"

"You sound like you ready to give the game up or something," Malek said, trying his best to read Joe, not sure whether he was taking a temporary break or if this was his way of weaning himself away from the game.

"I'm not giving up the game; I just want to take a little hiatus. Malek, I see a lot of myself in you. I see how you flip those bricks and run your blocks. You have cats twice your age respecting you, and you keep your whole crew happy. That's a hard task, family. You're a lot smarter than I was at nineteen, that's for sure. You got what it takes to be a great in this game. You just don't realize it yet. You got the 'shark complex,' just like I had."

"Shark complex?" Malek asked, totally puzzled.

Despite how anyone else on the streets saw Malek, he'd always pictured himself as just another member of the crew. Modest and humble in the game, he knew his place, which was actually why he was so respected. He didn't put on no act. What you saw with him was exactly what you got.

"Yeah, fam. A shark will die if it stops swimming. That's the way they breathe, the way they keep living, Malek. They have to keep moving to survive. That's how I look at life. I have to keep moving, keep progressing and stay on my grind, or I'm no more." Joe took a puff of his blunt, held it in for a moment, and then exhaled. "Ever since I was your age, I been a hustler, but everyone knows that this game doesn't last forever. At some point the head man gets death or jail. I feel that my fate is nearing. I need to fall back and let the new breeds spread their wings.

"Malek, you are the future. You are a boss in the making, and if I don't give you the opportunity, you are going to come for my spot and eventually have to kill me. You don't have to take the spot; I'ma give it to you." Joe looked into Malek's eyes. "I'm not going to make the same mistake with you that I made with Tariq."

Malek thought about what Jamaica Joe was doing. He was giving him something more valuable than money; he was giving him food for thought, and Malek was scraping the plate. What Joe was saying made a lot of sense to Malek, and he was soaking it in like a sponge. He was about to come into his own.

Jamaica Joe and Malek rode down Interstate 75 on their way to meet Joe's cocaine connect. Canada, just north of Detroit and only an hour and a half away from Flint, was their destination. Since the U.S. didn't allow planes from Colombia to land in the country, drug traffickers usually did business through Canada, so there was a lot of drug trafficking going on across the border.

Joe had been preparing Malek for this trip all week. He broke the game down to him and told him how the transactions went down. "I never ride dirty. I just go and negotiate the amount and price and then send a mule up to get the weight."

"So you drive all the way to Canada just to talk? Why wouldn't you just call?"

"That's not how we move, family. Drug transactions 101—no phones. Phones'll get you bagged. Every conversation and negotiation is made face-to-face with us—that's how you do business. Look a man in the face and handle yours. You have to use every precaution in this game, Malek, because you never know if and when them alphabet boys, the FBI and the DEA, are listening," Joe said as he reached the U.S.-Canada bridge.

The bridge was the only thing that separated Detroit from Canada, so they were in Detroit one minute and in Canada the next. Joe drove his black Ford Excursion into the public park just off the bridge.

Malek looked around in confusion, wondering why they were stopping there. He then began to look around, checking out the surroundings. He noticed a group of men sitting under a chess pavilion, paired off at various tables.

"This is where you find Fredro," Joe said, referring to his coke connect. He stepped out of the truck, closely followed by Malek, and they approached the pavilion.

Malek looked at the group of men they were walking up on, trying to guess which one might be Fredro. To Malek's surprise, Joe walked right past the group of men and approached the bench next to a raggedy-looking man wearing a dingy fishing hat. A slim-built African American man in his fifties with a full beard, he was pulling bread crumbs out of his pocket and tossing them to the birds. With the name Fredro, Malek was expecting an Italian, a Latino, or something—not a black man.

"Fredro, good afternoon," Joe said as he took a seat next to him.

"Good afternoon," Fredro replied in a deep, raspy voice, without taking his eyes off the pigeons that flocked to his crumbs.

"I want you to meet Malek. He is my man I was telling you about."

Malek stepped up into Fredro's view. "Nice to meet you," Malek said as he extended his hand.

Fredro shook Malek's hand and gave him a small grin. "I've heard a lot about you, Malek. I hear you're the future." Fredro threw another handful of crumbs.

Malek smiled and then glanced at Joe. "Oh, is that what they're saying?"

Joe began to discuss business with Fredro. "I need you to introduce me to some of your girls."

"How many?" Fredro asked, continuing to toss the breadcrumbs.

"I'm having a party. I need twenty of them."

"Twenty girls? That's a lot of girls, Joe."

"Well, my man Malek over here, he runs through them, feel me?"

"Yeah, I hear you."

"How old are they?" Joe asked, referring to the kilo price.

"They are all twenty-two. They're the best show-girls in the business," Fredro replied, still focusing on the birds before his feet.

"I'll send for them tomorrow night."

"Good," Fredro replied with a wink.

To the trained ear, a major drug deal had just gone down. Malek smiled at how they had just negotiated drug prices and quantity without mentioning any drugs. Jamaica Joe had schooled Malek about always talking indirectly to avoid incriminating himself. Malek was witnessing professionals at work.

"Fredro, like I was telling you, I'm taking a small vacation. My man Malek is going to be coming to see you in my place." Jamaica Joe nodded his head at Malek. "This li'l nigga is one hundred percent."

Fredro's facial expression immediately changed as he stood up and began to walk toward the lake. He was in obvious discomfort from Joe's news. Fredro had been pushing weight since the '80s and didn't like new people.

Jamaica Joe could read Fredro's mind. He whispered to Malek, "I'll be right back." Joe got up and went to catch up to Fredro.

Malek watched as the two men conversed in front of the lake. He couldn't make out what they were saying, but he was pretty confident about what they were discussing. Malek, too, could read the look on Fredro's face, but he knew he could prove himself if given the chance. "This nigga got to let me in," Malek whispered as he continued to eye the two men.

Just as he finished his thought, the men shook hands, and Joe headed back toward Malek. Jamaica Joe approached Malek and whispered, "You're in," as he brushed past him and headed back to his truck.

Malek couldn't help but smile. He had just achieved what D-boys around the country dreamed about. He was connected.

Chapter Eight

Two days after Jamaica Joe and Malek met with Fredro, Joe organized a meeting with his whole North Side crew to announce his absence, and also to introduce Malek as the head of the operations. He knew that he would ruffle some feathers with his street lieutenants by putting a nineteen-year-old at the boss position, but he had more confidence in Malek than any other worker.

Jamaica Joe sat at the head of the table in the back of one of the many businesses he owned, waiting to start. He watched Malek and observed his demeanor. *That li'l nigga right there is built for the game,* he thought as he lit a blunt.

Joe took his time before addressing his crew. Once he was ready, he stood up with Malek next to him. "As you all know, I'm taking a little break from the game. And before anybody gets it twisted, no, I ain't leaving the game. It's just like I said—I'm gon' fall back for a minute."

Joe scanned the room, looking everyone dead in the eyes to make sure they all got the point. The last thing he wanted was some false rumor floating around about him being out of the game. Niggas still needed to know that he ran the North Side.

"Everything will be the same," he informed them, "and business will continue as usual. The rules of the game have not changed. The only thing that will be different is that from now on"— He looked over at Malek like a proud father— "you'll put all your orders in with Malek. He will be filling in for me for a while."

The mood of the room changed suddenly with Joe's announcement. You could see the skepticism in the hustlers' faces upon hearing that Malek would now be the head man. Everyone in the room expected Tariq to be next in command, but they didn't know that he was no longer breathing.

Rumors were flying about Tariq's sudden disappearance, though. Some were saying that he ran off to New York or somewhere with Jamaica Joe's money to start his own crew. Some were saying that he got caught up in a bad run.

The cops hadn't found his body yet, so Joe decided to just let the rumors fly. He didn't have anything to gain by slandering Tariq's name and letting everyone know that he was a snake.

Looking back on the situation, Joe was man enough to take partial blame for Tariq's betrayal. He figured that Tariq had felt his own loyalty to Joe had already been betrayed when Joe brought Malek in the game. So Joe felt that he at least owed Tariq that much, to just let the nigga die without spittin' venom. Still, he didn't condone Tariq's acts and would send him to his death all over again if he had to.

Malek took the silence for what it was—doubt. Although usually laid-back and quiet, if he was gonna be in charge, some things needed to change. He needed to let these cats know that he could handle the position. "I see how niggas looking at me . . . like I can't handle this position, but I'ma tell y'all like this"—Malek pulled out his gun—"Take silver or take lead, straight the fuck up!"

Jamaica Joe smiled as he witnessed Malek begin to implement the tactics he'd broken down to him on how to run an organization. He was telling them to take silver (get money with him) or take lead (take his bullets).

Malek continued, "So you have two options. You can leave right now and become my enemy"—He scoped out every soldier in the room with an intense look in his eyes—"or you can stay and get money with me. Honestly, I'm cool with either. Choose one." Once again, Malek scanned the room, individually looking each hustler in his face.

Joe looked in Malek's eyes and saw sincerity. Malek wasn't saying something just to be saying it. He was ready to get at any nigga who went against the grain. At that moment, Joe knew he'd made the right decision in handing the operation over to him temporarily.

Nobody in the room moved as a brief moment of silence took place. The torch had just been passed.

Finally, Malek broke the silence and said, "Okay, let's get it then." He reached under the table and grabbed the oversized duffle bag, plopped it on the table, and opened it up. Inside the bag was twenty kilos of pure "unstepped-on" cocaine. Malek began to distribute the weight to the hustlers for them to supply their sections of the North Side.

After a brief meeting, the hustlers greeted Malek with respect and exited the room.

Jamaica Joe felt confident in splitting for a minute. He knew that if he stayed in town, the feds would eventually get him caught up in some bullshit, so for him it was the perfect time to take a break.

Once everyone left, only Joe and Malek sat at the table. Joe told his protégé, "Malek, this is a different game now. You are the man."

"I'm ready," Malek assured him, chin up and chest poked out.

Joe admired how Malek immediately put on the full armor of boss status, attitude and all. "I know you are, fam, but there are a lot of rules to this shit, and each one must be followed with precision. The last thing you need is for any mu'fucka to catch you slippin', 'cause, remember, there's always gon' be another nigga out there who wants your spot."

Malek nodded his head and listened closely as Joe gave him the game.

"With your new position, there'll be new responsibilities. You can't show weakness at all. Weakness will get you killed. Never let a nigga slide with anything. If you gotta put yo' murder game down, then so be it. Remember one thing—fear is much more powerful than love. If the streets love you, they could use that love to eventually sabotage you. Love never lasts forever. The streets build you up only to bring you down. But fear"—Joe took a puff from his blunt, which had burned on its own more than he'd smoked on it—"fear lasts forever."

Malek listened to Joe and was surprised at how Joe had the streets down to a science. He spoke on the streets as if he were Socrates discussing psychology.

For the next hour, Joe gave Malek a crash course on being a kingpin. He explained to Malek that it was his time, and informed him about the big birthday bash/ farewell party he was going to throw.

"I want to celebrate with the city before my departure, ya dig?" Joe said as he finished up his blunt and conversation with Malek.

Chapter Nine

Tasha awoke and went to her brother's room. She opened the door and noticed that Halleigh was still sleeping in his bed. *What the hell is she still doing in Maury's bed?* She was sure that by now Halleigh would have figured out that the room she'd been playing Goldilocks in was her brother's room, and copped one of the other rooms. But there Halleigh lay, sound asleep. Tasha shook her head and turned to leave, but found Mimi standing behind her, peering over her shoulder.

"What are we looking at?"

"Nothing. I was just checking to see if Hal was still asleep. Come on, let's go get some food."

They walked into the kitchen to find Maury coming into the house with bags in his hands.

"Maury!" Tasha yelled excitedly as she ran to hug him.

"Tasha, hold up, before you make me drop my food," he stated as he set the bags down on the countertop. He then turned around and hugged his sister warmly. "Why you didn't let me know you were coming to town?"

"I didn't even know I was coming. It was spur-of-the-moment, so I decided to surprise you."

"Umm-hmm." Mimi cleared her throat loudly as she eyed the sexy man before her. *Tasha ain't tell me her brother was so damn fine.* She put on her game face and stood sexily in the stretch pants and camisole she'd worn to bed.

"Oh yeah, this is my girl, Mimi. Mimi, this is my brother, Maury."

Maury licked his lips and gave Mimi a head nod. He'd already peeped the way she was checking for him when he first walked in. "What up, ma? It's nice to meet you," he said with a smile.

"It's nice to meet you too," Mimi replied sweetly.

Tasha rolled her eyes. She knew that Mimi was attracted to her brother when she heard her "get-'em" voice.

"You've already met Halleigh," Tasha interjected before Mimi could spark a conversation. She added, "And why did you sleep on your couch last night?"

"Because shorty stole my room," Maury replied with a sexy grin. He pulled two containers of food from a bag.

"You bought us breakfast?" Tasha asked.

"Nah, sis, you know your way around town, baby. This is for me," he said, backpedaling out the room.

Tasha frowned when she noticed he had two boxes.

"Well, who is that other one for?" she asked.

"This is for your girl. Since y'all left her on

'stuck' last night, I decided to buy her breakfast,"
Maury replied.

"Uh-huh." Tasha knew that Halleigh must have
worked her magic on Maury, because his nose was
wide open. She shook her head and watched him
walk out of the room. "Oh yeah, Maury, I need to
talk to you about something. It's important, so
make some time for me today!" she yelled.

"A'ight, I hear you!" he hollered back.

When he was out of earshot, Mimi tapped
Tasha's arm. "What the hell was that all about?
He's buying her breakfast and shit, like they
fucked last night."

Tasha could hear the jealousy in Mimi's voice.
She'd peeped Mimi eye-fucking her brother too
and knew that Mimi had her eyes set on a prize.

"You know Hal don't even get down like that.
It's nothing. I'm sure it's nothing at all."

Good, Mimi thought, '*cause a bitch like me sure can
make something out of nothing.*

Maury knocked on the bedroom door lightly.
He didn't want to wake Halleigh if she wasn't already up, but he entered the room anyway when
he didn't receive an answer. He walked near the
side of the bed and placed the food on the night-
stand.

"Yo, shorty, wake up," he whispered, nudging
her shoulder gently.

Halleigh heard the male voice, and in her head
she imagined that it was Manolo. She'd just had a
nightmare that Manolo was on top of her, smoth-
ering her with his body, his hand over her mouth

as she tried to scream for him to stop. In her nightmare, Manolo was raping her, and had been, every morning, to teach her obedience. Maury's voice had managed to blend into her nightmare.

"Your food is gon' get cold," Maury said, shaking her. "Wake up."

Halleigh slowly opened her eyes, and a feeling of unfamiliarity crept into her heart. She felt a pair of strong hands on her neck, and she immediately jumped up, thinking that it was Manolo touching her.

"Stop it! Get off of me! Manolo, please stop! Don't touch me!" She scrambled out of bed and peered frightfully at Maury.

"Whoa! Calm down, Halleigh. You're okay. It's just me," Maury said in a low, soothing tone.

Halleigh looked around slowly and began to realize where she was. This was one of the first mornings she was able to wake up without worrying about Manolo's treacherous ways. "He's gone," she whispered as she collapsed onto the bed and put her face in her hands. "He can't hurt you anymore," she told herself as her tears came unwillingly.

Maury didn't know who "he" was, but he knew that whoever Halleigh was referring to had terrified her to the breaking point. He walked over to the side of the bed and sat beside her. "You're good, ma. Ain't nobody gon' hurt you." He wrapped his arms around her.

Halleigh rested in his arms for a few minutes. It felt so safe and reassuring. There was only one pair of arms that ever felt like that around her—Malek's. Halleigh closed her eyes and envisioned

Malek there rescuing her from the horrible life she'd been living. She never wanted him to let her go.

Halleigh put her arms around Maury and pulled him closer to her. *Oh, Malek*, she thought as she pressed her face against him. Just then she looked up and saw Maury staring down at her. She quickly pulled away from him and walked into the bathroom and closed the door behind her, leaving a confused Maury on the bed.

Tears filled Halleigh's eyes as she began to whimper. "He can't hurt you anymore," she told herself. "You run your own shit now. Your life is in your hands, and you won't allow anyone to make you feel powerless again."

Halleigh got a piece of tissue from the toilet paper roll and wiped the last tear from her face, promising herself that she would stay strong. She needed to take control of her life, and she decided that today was the day she would start and never look back again.

She splashed cold water on her face, dried her hands, and then walked back out into the bedroom. Maury was still sitting on the bed. Halleigh saw that he had breakfast spread out on a small tray for her.

"I didn't know what you wanted," Maury said to Halleigh as he nodded toward the spread, "so I got you a little bit of everything."

Halleigh gave Maury a smile that said, "Thank you." She then lowered her head. She was sure that he would want an explanation for what he'd just witnessed from her a few minutes ago, but to her surprise, he didn't mention it. She was grateful for that as she stood there looking down at the food, wondering why he was being so nice to her. Nobody was kind for no reason, not at first anyway. They always wanted something. Halleigh wondered just what it was Maury wanted from her.

"Come here," Maury stated. He got up and walked toward Halleigh and grabbed her hand. "What's wrong? Never seen sausage and pancakes before?" Maury tried to lighten the awkward mood.

"Yeah." Halleigh nodded. "But what's it for?" she asked as she followed him toward the bed.

"What do you mean, what is it for? For you to eat." He pulled back the plush comforter for her.

She sat down, and he put some pillows behind her back.

"I mean, what's up with you bringing me breakfast in bed?"

He placed the breakfast tray on her lap. "Just enjoy it, shorty. But don't get used to it. I don't do this for everybody, you know. But you deserve it for putting up with me and my gangster movies last night."

Halleigh looked around the room. "Well, how did I even get in this bed last night?" she asked, knowing that he had to have carried her to bed. She couldn't help but appreciate the gesture. If she had been at another point in her life, Tasha's brother could have easily had her open, but she could barely keep Malek off her mind, so she knew she didn't have the energy to spark something with Maury.

"I brought you in here after you passed out on me."

Her eyebrows rose inquisitively. "And where did you sleep?"

Maury laughed out loud at her facial expression. "Chill out, shorty. I crashed on the couch."

"Well, thank you for the breakfast, Maury, and for sharing your bed with me."

"You don't have to thank me, Halleigh." Maury grabbed the bag with his own food and left the room.

Mimi waited near the room she'd slept in until she saw Maury emerge from the room where Halleigh was. She was now dressed in tight jeans that showed off her apple bottom. She wore no bra, so her nipples peered at Maury through her thin halter top.

"Hey, Maury," she stated as he walked toward her. She grabbed his hand and stopped him from moving past her. She walked up close to him and blatantly rubbed her body against him.

"What up, ma?" He looked her up and down.

Mimi's body was on point, and he felt his manhood jump in excitement, but he had to check himself. This was one of his sister's peoples. Besides, he knew Mimi's type. She was out for a quick-dick fix and he knew it. On top of that, he was almost certain that it would cost him some paper in the end, whether it was flat-out cash or an afternoon shopping spree. Mimi's type came with a price.

Now, Maury definitely felt that Mimi was worth fucking, but he could see straight through her. She could never be wifey. Like any man, he'd keep his options open, but for now, he'd have to put her on reserve.

"You tell me what's up," Mimi said seductively. She could see that Maury's eyes were focused on her breasts. "You want to touch?" she ran her tongue across her front teeth . . . slowly.

By now, Maury's dick was rock-hard, and her offer was tempting, but he shook his head. "Nah, ma, maybe some other time."

He tried to walk away, but Mimi pulled him back toward her and into the room.

"What you doing, ma?" he asked. His breath caught in his throat as he put his hands in the air to avoid touching her.

Mimi didn't answer, but she grabbed his hands and put them on her breasts.

"What, what you doing, girl?" Maury said, attempting to push her away.

Mimi knew damn well that Maury could overpower her any day of the week. If he really wanted her to back up off of him, he'd be using much more force than he was. She put her hands on top of Maury's and began directing them to caress her. She let out a soft moan.

Eventually, Maury couldn't help himself. He began massaging Mimi's D-cups without her assistance, circling his thumbs around her stiff nipples.

"Ummm," Mimi moaned in his ear. "I knew you wanted to touch them." Mimi took one of Maury's hands, removed it from her breast, and put it up her shirt.

"Damn, girl," Maury let slip out. He didn't want Mimi to know that he was that into it, but now the cat was out of the bag. Maury closed the bedroom door, lifted her shirt, and picked her up so that he could bury his head in her chest.

One by one, back and forth, forth and back, Maury plucked at Mimi's nipples with his tongue. Her nipples tasted like honey as he licked all over them, sucking them aggressively.

She reached down and felt his manhood and then pushed him against the door.

"Damn," he whispered.

Mimi got down on her knees while unzipping Maury's jeans. She released his penis from his pants and put it in her mouth. She didn't play with it or hesitate, but deep-throated him with passion as she cupped his balls in her soft hands.

"Oh shit," he stated as he gripped the back of her head and ground his hips into her as if he were fucking her pussy. He didn't want to fuck with Mimi like that, not now, but her seduction was irresistible as he looked down at his dick disappearing over and over again into her mouth.

Fuck what you've read, Superhead didn't have shit on Mimi, as far as Maury was concerned.

Mimi moved from his dick to his balls, pleasing him with her tongue, while she massaged her hand up and down his shaft.

Tingles shot from Maury's toes to his upper spine, and he curled his toes in delight.

Mimi had mastered the art of sucking dick a long time ago and was giving Maury her all.

Maury didn't know what it was that Mimi wanted out of all this when all was said and done, but any broad who could suck dick like a champ the way Mimi was doing deserved whatever the fuck she wanted.

"I'm about to nut, ma," he whispered. "Put it back in your mouth," he instructed.

Mimi followed his orders, and thirty seconds later, he let off.

"Ughh!" he moaned as his body jerked. Maury had expected Mimi to let his semen drip to the floor, but to his surprise, she swallowed every ounce of him and licked his dick clean before tucking it back into his pants where it belonged.

Mimi smiled proudly as she stood back to her feet.

She attempted to kiss him on the lips, but he discreetly turned his head, and she caught his cheek. *I don't know where this bitch mouth been,* he thought. He had to give her credit, though—she had a mean head game.

"You gon' get with me?" Mimi asked him.

"Yeah, I'll get with you," he lied. He instantly began to regret fucking around with Mimi. He knew he had no intention of getting to know her better, and he was hoping that he hadn't led her on. *Fuck it! We both grown as hell. Bitch shouldn't have put herself out there like that if she doesn't want a nigga to take advantage.*

He opened the door and headed to the living room to go eat his food, but then he decided that he wanted to take a shower. He'd just have to warm his food up in the microwave afterward. Maury headed toward his room and knocked, slowly pushing it open.

Halleigh smiled when she saw him poke his head in first and then step into the room.

Upon seeing her pretty, innocent-like smile, Maury's conscience immediately began to fuck with him. He was trying to get at Halleigh, yet he'd just let one of her best friends suck his dick. He decided then and there that he would keep Mimi at arm's length and try to get close to Halleigh, hoping he hadn't completely destroyed his chances.

"I need to get in here," he stated.

"It's your room." Halleigh shrugged as she chewed up the forkful of pancakes she'd just stuffed in her mouth. "Go ahead and handle your business. I need to go kick Tasha's ass anyway for not coming back for me yesterday like she said she would." Halleigh bit a piece of sausage and then hopped out of the bed and gathered up the mess she'd made. She walked toward the door, but before leaving the room she turned and said, "Maury?"

"What's good, shorty?" he replied as he looked at Halleigh, who immediately put her head down.

"Thank you for not pushing the issue this morning about how I acted and all, you know, when you came to bring me my food. I know I spazzed out on you. I'm sorry."

"It's not my place to push you to do or say anything that you don't feel comfortable with. When and if you're ready to talk, I would like to know more about you, including the reason why you spazzed out, and why you never look me in the eye when I talk to you."

Halleigh nodded and replied, "Maybe one day we can kick it, just not today." She left the room in search of Tasha and found her sitting on the living room couch, channel-surfing.

Halleigh plopped down beside Tasha. "What happened to you yesterday?"

"Girl, you know how Mimi is. Act like she ain't never been nowhere in her life," Tasha said, rolling her eyes. "Mimi's ass was dragging me all over town. We did the whole tourist thing down on Canal, buying all the knock-off shit. Then we stopped off in this little spot and had a couple drinks. By the time we made it back to the house, it was late. Sorry, girl. We wasn't trying to leave you here by yourself."

"It's nothing. I was too tired to be going out anyway. Plus, your brother hooked me up with some dinner last night." Halleigh turned to face Tasha. "You know, your brother is real chill. I like him."

"What? You talking about another nigga besides that lame Malek?"

"I didn't mean I *liked* him liked him. I just meant that he's cool people, is all."

Halleigh's mood immediately turned somber, and Tasha regretted letting the words come from her mouth. "I'm sorry, Hal. I wasn't thinking."

"It's all right. I'm good." Halleigh leaned back against the couch and let out a deep sigh, her mind filled with thoughts of Malek. "I do miss him, though, Tasha," she confessed. "I just can't ever be down with him again. I mean, how could he be fucking with the niggas that raped me? Why would he do that to me?" Halleigh asked, her voice low. "Is this his way of paying me back for hooking up with Manolo? I mean, I know it hurts him that I ended up doing what I do for a living—"

"Stop it right there," Tasha said, sitting up on the couch and facing Halleigh. "What you *used* to do. You are not a Manolo Mami anymore. That shit's in the past, do you hear me?"

"Yeah." Halleigh nodded as Tasha relaxed herself

back on the couch. "But even so, why would Malek do that to me?"

"I don't know, Hal. I don't know. But fuck him! You don't need that type of drama in your life. You have sixty-five hundred dollars to start a new life with, and once I talk to Maury about these bricks, you gon' have way more than that. Manolo's gone, fuck Malek. It's all about us."

"I know," Halleigh replied. "It is about us now, ain't it?" she said with a weak smile.

"Now on to more important things. What did you do to my brother?" Tasha quizzed excitedly.

Halleigh pulled back with a puzzled look on her face. "What are you talking 'bout? I ain't do nothing. He's just cool peoples, that's all. We're cool."

"Just cool, huh. Got my cheap-ass brother buying you dinner and breakfast and shit. The same brother who made me pay his ass back if I borrowed a nickel from him to buy penny candy, and you say, 'Just cool'? Humpf."

"Girl, I'm serious. Nothing happened," Halleigh assured her, nudging her on the arm playfully. "Unless you call me falling asleep something."

"Whatever. I know you lying, but that's okay," Tasha replied. "It's time to handle this business anyway." Tasha threw the remote down on the couch and got up. "Where is Maury?"

"He's in his room, eating or getting something," Halleigh replied. "I'm not sure, but he was in his room when I left out of there."

Tasha shot Halleigh a mischievous look. "Mm-hmm, and nothing happened."

Halleigh laughed. "Will you cut it out already?"

Tasha walked toward the hallway and called out, "Mimi, bring the bag out here!" and then returned to the couch next to Halleigh.

Mimi came waltzing in the room with a smug expression on her face as she carried the bag in her hand. She handed it off to Tasha and sat down in the chair across from her friends.

Tasha took the kilos of cocaine out of the bag and spread it out across the table. "Look, let me do all the talking, a'ight?"

"Okay," Mimi responded, and Halleigh just nodded her head in agreement.

"Hal, go grab Maury," Tasha said.

Halleigh got up and headed down the hallway toward the back of the house. She knocked on his bedroom door.

"It's open," he yelled.

Halleigh opened the door to find Maury standing in sweatpants with no shirt on, his upper body still wet from his shower. Her eyes admired his chiseled chest and abs for a quick second.

He smirked. "What's up, shorty?"

"Um, we need to talk to you in the living room," Halleigh said, shaking her head and diverting her eyes from his body.

Maury grabbed his shirt from the bed and started walking toward Halleigh. As he approached her, he noticed that she began to tense up. As a matter of fact, it seemed as though every time he got near her she tensed up.

Malek had been the only man ever to cause this type of feeling to come over her, so Halleigh didn't know what to make of it. The closer Maury got to her, the more chills ran up her body, causing her to tremble slightly. She quickly allowed her eyes to roam from Maury's perfect physique down to the floor.

By that time, Maury was all up in her personal space, placing his index finger underneath her chin and lifting her head so that she was now face to face with him.

"I can't see this pretty face of yours if you're looking down at your feet all the time," he whispered.

Halleigh couldn't help but crack a smile as she looked into his eyes. "Is this better?" she asked with a corny grin.

He laughed and replied, "Yeah, that's better." He slipped his shirt over his head, keeping his eyes glued on her the entire time. He then reached out his arm and stated, "Go ahead, I'm following you."

Maury put his hand on the small of Halleigh's back as she walked in front of him. It was a slight gesture of affection that Halleigh didn't even really make notice of, but Mimi saw it as soon as they came into clear view.

What the fuck? Mimi's insides began to boil, she was so angry. She was the one who had just given up the goodies to Maury, been on her knees, pleasing this fool, and now he wanted to spit in her face by toting Halleigh into the room like she was Beyoncé and Mimi was Kelly or, even worse, Michelle.

She looked over at Tasha to see if she noticed it, but Tasha didn't seem to be fazed. Mimi straightened her shoulders with confidence, checked herself out, and refocused on the task at hand.

When Maury noticed his table filled with cocaine, he stopped dead in his tracks. "Fuck you get this from?" he asked, looking directly at Tasha.

"Manolo," Tasha replied.

"Manolo?" It was the same name he'd heard Halleigh say earlier when she panicked in his room. His brow creased in disapproval. He had a feeling that his sister had not come by the product on good terms with the original owner. "Who the fuck is Manolo, and what do his bricks got to do with me?"

"They're not his bricks anymore," Tasha answered. "They're ours." Tasha looked to Mimi and Halleigh.

"Yeah," Mimi said, "and we need you to get these off for us."

Maury looked at Mimi as if she were crazy, but Tasha quickly cut in. "Of course, we'll give you a cut, Maury. I know better than to ask you to work for free."

Maury looked at Halleigh, who was still standing by his side, and shook his head. He would never have guessed she was in the dope game. Her looks were deceiving, and he made a mental note of that.

"How'd you get 'em, Tash?" Maury asked, ready to get to the bottom of things. Whenever someone wanted to come out on top, there had to be a bottom somewhere. He was determined to find out just what it was, before getting himself involved.

Tasha didn't want to inform her brother of all the details surrounding how she'd come to gain possession of the bricks. She definitely didn't want him to know that she'd snitched on Manolo, but she knew that she couldn't lie to him. If he was going to be a part of their hustle, she didn't want him going in blind, setting himself up for the okey-doke.

Tasha took a deep breath and then started. "I set the nigga up to get caught with the dope and then cut a deal with the arresting officer."

"You did what?" Maury asked, enraged. "You know the game, baby! Fuck is you doing?" He shook his head from side to side. "Fuck was you thinking? You out in the Midwest by yourself, but you want to stick a nigga for his bricks? If the nigga would have come back at you, what was gon' happen then?"

"I'm not even trying to hear all that you talking," Tasha said, folding her arms like a pretzel, poking out her lips, and then looking away. She didn't want to hear what baby bro had to say because she knew it wasn't going to be anything other than what she already knew to be the truth. "Look, I didn't have a choice, Maury!" Tasha said in her own defense, hoping to get her brother to understand.

Maury just stood there shaking his head at his sister's stupidity.

"Don't look at me like that, nigga," Tasha spat. "By hook or by crook is what you always taught me, so don't be frowning your shits up at me now! And Manolo ain't coming back at me, 'cause his ass is sitting in somebody's jail cell right now!" Tasha yelled.

"I don't even know you right now, Tash. I know

you know better. I know you know. And then you pull Charlie's Angels into your mess with you," he said, referring to Mimi and Halleigh.

The girls all just stood there in silence, waiting for Maury to finish up his rant so that they could hear his final word—was he going to help them unload the bricks or not?

Maury sighed and covered his face with his hands. He thought for a moment and then slid his hands down his face. "Look, sis, let me clear my head before I say some shit that I might regret," he said as he turned and left the room.

"Maury!" she called, but her voice was matched by the sound of a slamming door.

"Fuck is his problem?" Mimi asked. "He shouldn't be worried about how we got 'em. The point is, they sitting on his living room table. Is he gon' help us get this cash or not?"

"I don't know what he's going to do." Tasha threw her arms up in the air and allowed them to collapse to her side in defeat. "I can't even talk to him right now. I don't know what I was thinking. He never listens to me anyway. For some reason he's always thought that he was the oldest and could tell me what the fuck to do and how to do it."

Tasha thought back to their childhood and how people used to just assume he was the oldest because of the way he always had his stuff together. Tasha was just the opposite. When an idea came into her mind, she just did it and hoped for the best. It was pretty much the same reasoning she used in setting up Manolo. As far as she was concerned, her instincts had not failed her yet, so she was going to keep sticking to them, no matter how foolish her brother thought they were.

"Well, time is money," Mimi spat. "Either your brother is in, or he ain't. And if he ain't, time is wasting. We need to move on to someone who will help us. Or like the old saying goes, if we want the shit done right, maybe we need to do it our damn selves."

"You're right, Mimi. Time is money, and time is a-wasting, but I can't talk to him right now. He's fired up, so I know some slick shit is going to come out of his mouth, and in turn, something slick is going to come out of my mouth. That's the story of me and my brother's life." Tasha then had a sudden thought. "Halleigh, you go talk to him."

"Me? Why the hell I got to talk to him? He's *your* brother." The last thing Halleigh wanted was to have to get close to Maury again. Besides, she didn't know what to say.

"Exactly. He ain't gon' do nothing but yell at me and tell me how disappointed he is for me snitching. But, hell, he likes you. He brought you breakfast in bed, didn't he? So, who knows? He might actually listen to you. And if you ain't learned nothing else in these last couple of years, it's the power of your pussy."

"Oh, hell no!" Halleigh started. "If you think I'm gonna—"

"That's not what I'm trying to say, Hal," Tasha told her. "Come on, you know me better than that. I'm not telling you to sleep with him just to get him to help us. I'm just saying that he likes you, and because he likes you, he'll probably listen to you. Okay?"

Halleigh thought for a minute and then nodded her head. "All right. You've had my back on more than one occasion," Halleigh told Tasha. "This is the least I can do."

"Thanks, Hal," Tasha said.

Halleigh headed back to Maury's room.

She knocked, but didn't wait for him to invite her in before she opened the door and stepped into the room. "Can we talk?" Halleigh asked Maury, who was lying on his bed, his hands behind his head.

He nodded, giving her the okay.

Halleigh closed the door behind her, walked over, and sat down on his bed.

"What up?" he asked.

"I need to tell you something."

"Look, I don't want to hear all the details of this bullshit y'all done let my sister talk y'all into."

"No, wait. It's not about that," Halleigh told him.

"Then what's it about?"

"It's about, it's about me. Well, really about all of us," Halleigh told him. "I know you don't know everything there is to know about the life the three of us were living in Flint. I know because it's something that Tasha was too ashamed to tell you herself." Halleigh couldn't believe that she was getting ready to share her troubles with Maury, whom she'd known less than forty-eight hours. She paused and took a deep breath.

"I'm listening," he said, urging her to continue.

"Have you ever heard of Malek Johnson?"

Without even having to think about it, Maury replied, "Yeah, I heard of dude. That nigga should have been the next LeBron James, but then he turned around and got on some stupid shit." Maury shook his head. "What a waste. He was supposed to be the number one draft pick, what was it, about two years ago, right?"

Halleigh closed her eyes and nodded. She couldn't help but be reminded of what could have been for Malek if she hadn't been in his life. He had everything going for him, and in a matter of a few hours and a stupid decision, it was all snatched away. *And all because of me*, she reminded herself.

"Well, he is my ex-boyfriend. We were supposed to get married right after the draft, but we never made it that far."

"It's a shame. He could have had millions, and he jeopardized it all for some chump change he pulled from a petty robbery. I don't care if they did find him not guilty. Everybody knows that nigga did that shit. He just happened to have the best criminal lawyer money could buy. Hell, if you ask me, they even paid for that witness he—"

"Look, that's not where I'm trying to go with all this," Halleigh said, putting her hand up to halt Maury's words. "But, for the record, everything Malek might have done or might not have done was for me. See, the night he got arrested for that robbery, he had won the championship game. As a reward to him from me"—Halleigh put her head down and blushed before continuing—"I had planned on giving him my virginity." Halleigh tried her hardest to keep from crying as she relived that awful night. "That night, after the game, he dropped me off at my house so that I could go change clothes and freshen up. I was supposed to meet him back at his house afterward. But, un-known to me, there would be a change of plans."

Her voice cracking, Halleigh continued, "That night, before I could make it out of the front door to get to his house, something went down between my mother and her dealer. The next thing I know, I'm being held down and raped in exchange for my mom's drugs."

Maury stammered, "I, uh, I'm—"

"It's okay," Halleigh told him. "I'm over it now, but back then I never wanted to talk to my mother again, let alone live under the same roof with her, so I ran. I ran to the only safe place I knew, and that was in Malek's arms. He offered me a place to rest my head at his house, but when his mother came home and found us in bed together, she flipped out. We tried to explain that we hadn't done anything, that we hadn't disrespected her home like that, but she wasn't trying to hear it, so she threw me out. Right there in the middle of the night in the pouring rain, she threw me out into the streets."

"Let me guess," Maury said. "Malek decided to go with you?"

Halleigh nodded. "Yep, he loved me so much that he chose me over his mother. The biggest mis-take he ever made in his life."

Halleigh continued to explain how Malek had robbed a store that night in an attempt to get money for a hotel for her, but he'd been caught and arrested before he could barely step foot out of the store. She also told him how she'd met Mimi and was invited back to her house to meet Mimi's father, who ended up being Manolo, her pimp.

Maury couldn't believe all of the things she'd been through. She told him how Manolo had starved her for days, beat her mercilessly, and degraded her often. Halleigh told Maury how she was about to kill herself, until Tasha promised her a way out.

"Tasha would've never snitched on Manolo if she wasn't trying to help me," Halleigh explained.

Maury looked into Halleigh's eyes. Tears had begun to flow down her cheeks, and he wiped them away. Her story might have turned off most dudes, because they would view her as nothing more than a ho. But he viewed her as a survivor and immediately felt a connection to her that he'd never felt for any other chick in his life. Even though she was only nineteen and he was twenty-five, he was drawn to Halleigh. She had already lived well past her years. She had seen much and been through enough to last her a lifetime.

"So, y'all really need me to move those bricks for y'all, huh?" he asked, his tone revealing that his answer was going to be yes.

She nodded her head. "Yes, Maury, we really need you to do this for us." Halleigh grabbed his hands and held them in hers. For the first time, she wasn't shaking or nervous. Her future, her girls' futures, relied on Maury turning that dope into cash so that they could start life over, a life that didn't include having to sell their bodies.

"Please . . . I don't ever want to live that life again, and neither does your sister." Halleigh thought for a moment and decided to break the tension with a little joke. "Now, Mimi, on the other hand . . ."

Halleigh and Maury shared a slight chuckle.

Maury got serious again. He stared into Halleigh's eyes. This time Halleigh saw a strong passion in his eyes. That made her nervous.

Before she could turn her head away, Maury leaned into her, and she tensed up again. He shook his head and said, "I'm not Manolo, Halleigh. I won't hurt you."

He kissed her lips softly, and she kissed him gently, until she realized what she was doing. Then she quickly pulled away.

"Wait, Maury," she said as she wiped her hands across her lips. "I can't do this with you right now. I still have mixed emotions about Malek, and I'm still trying to find out who I am as a woman. I was seventeen when my childhood was taken from me, but I never knew how to be a woman. Now I can finally control my own life, and I don't know what direction I need to go in. I have to find myself before I can give you anything," she said sadly.

"No, you don't, ma. You don't have to find yourself. You are who you are, and I'm willing to accept you for just that. And I don't want anything from you. If anything, I want to be the one to give you whatever it is that you need," he replied. He kissed her lips again and then said, "But I'll respect you as a woman and wait until you're ready." Maury knew Halleigh was special from the moment he'd first met her, but now after hearing her story, he felt she was even more special. He had to admit that he felt sorry for her, for the life she'd been forced to endure. Something inside of him just wanted to make up for all the wrong that had been done to her.

Halleigh wrapped her arms around him. "Thank you," she said. She stood to her feet and wiped her eyes.

"Send Tasha in here," Maury said.

"Okay," Halleigh replied as she turned to leave the room. Having a sudden thought, she turned back around and said, "Maury, about what I told you about how we worked for Manolo and all—"

"Don't worry," he said, cutting her off. "If Tasha wants to tell me, then I'll let her, but if not"—He put his finger over his lips, letting Halleigh know that it would be their little secret.

Halleigh smiled and then exited the room. She felt that it was Tasha's right to tell her brother the life she'd been living in Flint. When she walked back into the living room, Mimi was sitting on the living room couch and biting her nails impatiently, while Tasha was pacing back and forth.

Mimi was the first to spot Halleigh. "Well, what did he say?" she asked eagerly.

Tasha stopped pacing. "Is he going to help us or not?"

Halleigh just stood there looking at both girls, each with her own look of desperation covering her face. She sighed deeply and then stared down to the floor.

Both Tasha's and Mimi's shoulders slumped as they, too, sighed. Tasha threw her arms up in defeat and went to turn around, but before she could do so, Halleigh said, "He said yes!"

"What?" Tasha said, making sure she'd heard Halleigh right.

"He said yes. He'll do it," Halleigh replied.

"Gotcha." Halleigh pointed to both of the girls and laughed.

"Girl," Tasha said, play-hitting Halleigh.

Mimi gave a sigh of relief. "Damn it, Hal, you almost made my heart stop. Don't play like that." Mimi put her hand over her heart and sat down on the couch.

"Sorry, girls. I couldn't resist," Halleigh said. She looked to Tasha. "Tash, he wants to speak with you."

Tasha playfully rolled her eyes at Halleigh and then gave her a little nudge as she passed by her, heading to her brother's room. Before completely exiting the room, Tasha turned to Halleigh. "What exactly did you say to him to get him to help us out?"

Halleigh looked down and began to stutter. "I–I, uh, you know, just told him some things about me, the life I was living with Manolo." Halleigh paused and looked up at Tasha. "And, you know, how badly we need his help and all."

Without Halleigh saying another word, Tasha figured that if Halleigh told Maury the lifestyle she was living with Manolo, then he'd probably already put two and two together and figured out that she'd been living the same lifestyle. Tasha simply gave Halleigh a look of understanding and then headed back toward Maury's bedroom.

Chills went up her spine as she thought about what her brother would think of her now. Would he look at her the same? How would he feel now, knowing that his older sister, the one he was supposed to look up to, the one who was supposed to set an example for him, was a whore?

Now Tasha just wished she had told him a long time ago when she first got into the game, and gotten it over with. Now here she was, officially out of every aspect of the game, and yet she felt ashamed and dirty.

Up until just a few minutes ago, Tasha's brother thought she'd been living in Flint, working for a contract cleaning company. Tasha had told him that she was in charge of the employees. Seeing that she was in charge of all of the Manolo Mamis, she didn't feel as though she had completely lied to her brother. And, in addition to that, she knew that with her brother living in New York and her living in Flint, Michigan, he'd never find out the real deal. Nonetheless, the truth was out now, and she wasn't even the one to tell him.

A part of her wanted to be the one to tell her brother who she really was. But then there was another part of her that was glad Halleigh had removed the burden from her shoulders and had done it for her. So many times she'd wondered exactly how she would tell her brother that his sister was a whore. Now she didn't have to wonder any longer.

Tasha walked into Maury's bedroom and saw the pained look on his face, further confirmation that he knew the truth about his big sister.

"She told you, huh?" Tasha asked as she walked in and sat down beside Maury, dropping her head and staring down at her feet. She made a mental note that as soon as everything was smoothed over and business was taken care of, she'd treat herself to a pedicure.

"Yeah, but why didn't you tell me?" he asked.

Tasha shrugged her shoulders. "I guess I was just embarrassed that I allowed myself to get in that situation. I wanted to tell you so many times, Maury. Believe me, I did. But then I didn't know how to. I mean, how does a girl tell her brother that her boss is really a pimp?"

Maury shook his head and gritted his teeth. "The nigga better hope he get jail time, because I'ma get at his ass if he don't. I can't believe he was pimping my sister."

"If it makes you feel any better, and I know it probably won't, but he hasn't pimped me in years. I started out turning tricks, but then . . ." Tasha stopped as she thought about the brutal attack from one of her johns that put her in retirement from hoeing. "But then Manolo realized that I'd make him more money being in charge of the other girls, keeping them in line and straight."

"So you were, what, a madam or some shit?"

"Yeah, something like that."

"So did you know how bad he was treating the girls?"

Tasha remained silent, which was enough to answer Maury's question.

"I mean, some of the shit Halleigh was telling me went down . . . what kind of man treats women like that?" He continued shaking his head as he thought of the life that Halleigh had led. "I can't believe that monster treated shorty like that."

Tasha did a double-take. "Shorty? What about me?" Tasha asked with mock envy as she punched her brother's shoulder.

"Yeah, and you too," he added before his mind wandered off again to thoughts of Halleigh.

Tasha just came right out and asked her brother, "You like her, don't you?"

Blushing with embarrassment, Maury straightened himself up and said, "That's not important. Let's focus on getting this money." He held his fist up in a pound.

Tasha smiled and met his fist with hers. It was a handshake they had done since they were kids, and she knew that it meant he was down for the cause.

Tasha and Maury sat and talked about him unloading the bricks for them. And even though Tasha hadn't been the one to tell her brother the truth about the life she had been living, she did bring him up to speed with some of the other happenings in Flint.

Maury thought New York was off the hook, but he was beyond intrigued by what occurred in a little city in the Midwest, of all places. Who knew? In his opinion, Flint sounded more gutter than New York, and from what he was hearing, there were a few cats out in Flint getting money. He could definitely see the opportunity that was presenting itself.

Robbery was Maury's profession, so it wasn't like he was on the up-and-up in the life he was living either. But he had never kept it from his sister and had always shared everything with her. That's just how close they were, coming up. Heck, they used to use the same toothbrush sometimes. No matter what Maury got into, though, Tasha was always going to love him, the same way he still loved her.

Maury took the game of robbery to another level. It was a passion he had perfected. He had to be one of the most ruthless and notorious stick-up kids in New York City. He went from borough to borough, holding cats up for their paper. Ski-masking was his method, and he was living nice off his gains. Flint sounded like just the city for him. It was small and unsuspecting, just the way he liked it. *Yeah, I'm definitely about to see what Flint has to offer,* he thought as Tasha finished up her tales about the city.

" 'Spite what it sounds like, I do like Flint. Hell, my life is there." Tasha looked down at the clothes she was wearing, which were just some plain-Jane type of garments. She just grabbed what was easy when she and the girls had left town. "Hell, all my damn clothes are there too." She chuckled. "I worked too hard to just leave my shit for them other hoes to cop." Tasha thought for a minute. "Besides, I was thinking, the girls and I need to go back to Flint anyway."

"Why?" Maury asked.

"No one knows I set Manolo up, but if I just stay gone and shit, people are going to put two and two together. So I'm going to tell the girls that we need to go back just for a minute, so that we don't look so suspect. If people ask where we were, we'll just tell them we were laying low in a hotel somewhere, hiding from the cops." Tasha looked to Maury for a reaction to her reasoning. "So, what do you think?"

"Look, sis, I see what you're saying, and I agree.

But I can't let you go back to Flint by yourself, not after the hot shit you just pulled. As far as you know, that cop done turned on you by now. You could already be looking suspect. On the other hand, no one may suspect a thing and there might be more money to be made."

Maury looked off greedily. It was an expression Tasha had seen many times before in Mimi's eyes.

"I know that look," Tasha told him. "What are you thinking, little bro?"

"What I'm thinking is, that nigga Manolo probably got more than one safe." He looked at Tasha. "You said you set him up at the club? The police got him for his safe at the club?"

Tasha nodded.

"I'm sure that nigga got a safe at the crib."

Tasha hadn't really thought of that. She shrugged her shoulders.

"Yeah, if that nigga was a player in the game like you say he was, then I know he didn't stack all of his eggs in one basket. Bet you any amount of money that nigga got a stash where he lays his head."

"Maybe so, but right now, one bird in the hand is worth two in the bush. I'm trying to get paid off of the shit we got."

"All right, all right," Maury said, putting the idea of hitting up Manolo's crib on the back burner to simmer. "Tell you what, I'm going to get the bricks off here, and then in a couple days, we'll go back to Flint. I'd never forgive myself if some shit popped off and I could've prevented it from happening, so I'm gon' stick around your city for a while, just to make sure you're straight. Then if you decide you wanna roll back to the NY with me, you know you always got a place to rest your head."

Tasha nodded and reached out to hug her brother before she left the room. She was elated. In a couple of days, she would be twenty thousand dollars richer.

Chapter Ten

The next day, Maury hit the block to get the bricks off. Although the drug trade wasn't really his line of work, he knew a couple cats from around the way who were looking to buy some work, and he blessed them with the weight for $15,000 per brick. Since the going rate in New York was at least twenty-three G's, niggas flocked to the price, and the eight bricks were gone in a matter of hours. His pockets were $120,000 heavier, and after he split it with Tasha and her crew, he'd still have sixty stacks all to himself.

He made his way back to the crib, and when he arrived, he saw Halleigh sitting on his front stoop. He grabbed the duffle bag from his back seat, checked his hip to ensure that his pistol was in place, and checked his rearview mirror before exiting the '08 Lexus IS. He knew word had probably gotten out that he had moved some weight, and he was sure that somebody saw him as an opportunity to get paid. He may have been the most ruthless stick-up kid in town, but he wasn't the only one. And he knew the game. Had the shoe been on the other foot, he'd be waiting in the cut somewhere for his mark.

That was another reason why he knew it was a good idea to leave town and head to Flint with Tasha. He'd need to lay low. That way niggas would think he went on vacation and blew the money somewhere. His trip to Flint would give his hood a chance to settle down and forget that he'd ever made the large transactions.

Maury approached Halleigh and, as he walked past her, motioned his head toward the house. "Come inside. I need to holla at you about something," he told her as he stepped into the house.

Halleigh followed behind him until they reached the kitchen. Mimi and Tasha were chilling in the living room, and Maury quickly gathered them up too. He poured the duffle bag full of money out onto the kitchen table.

"Damn!" Mimi exclaimed. She had never seen so much money in her life. She jumped up and down excitedly. "I'm about to cop me a new whip as soon as we get back to Flint. I know Pookie who runs that car lot over on—"

"Stop talking stupid, Mimi," Tasha said, cutting her off. "Ain't none of us copping anything extravagant. What we look like, going back home with new cars and shit? That would make us look suspect as hell. We didn't have it before, so we ain't about to get it now. At least until we figure out a front that would explain us coming into some money. Besides, I don't plan on making Flint home again permanently. We need to stick around just long enough to make sure our names are good. You never know when you might need a muthafucka again. And if for some reason we were to make Flint home again, we want to make sure it's all good. You got that?"

Mimi shrugged, but in her mind, she was picturing a nice new candy apple red convertible.

"Go make sure the front door is locked," Tasha suddenly stated.

"I locked it," Maury told her.

"Go double check," Tasha insisted.

Mimi went and made sure the door was locked and then returned.

"This is a lot of money." Halleigh stared down at it in disbelief.

Manolo had made sure that she never saw more than a couple hundred dollars at a time. The less money he let the girls run around with, the more likely they were to be dependent upon him. In addition to that, he never gave the girls anymore than they'd need for their essentials. That way they couldn't stack up a nest egg to try to run off on him one day.

So, to Halleigh, having more than a hundred thousand in front of her was crazy. She knew that her life had just made a turn for the better as soon as Maury started dividing it up.

He took his cut first, which left the girls with $20,000 apiece.

"I can really start over with this much money," Halleigh stated happily.

Maury noticed her mood had changed instantly. It was as if a huge burden had been lifted off her shoulders, and it caused him to smile discreetly.

Tasha and Mimi peeped the way Maury was looking at Halleigh. Tasha smiled to herself. She'd never seen her brother react to a chick the way he was reacting to Halleigh.

Back when Tasha was younger, she would have kicked Halleigh to the curb, as her friend, before she could blink. She hated when she would bring her friends around Maury and he would get a little crush on them, but what she hated most was when the girls tried to holler at him behind her back. It was just an unspoken rule that friends don't date their friends' brothers. And Tasha, being as protective of her little brother as she was, just wasn't having it.

One time in particular, she had a best friend named Kera, whom she'd been tight with since fifth grade. Kera had come to the house and had sleepovers with Tasha on many occasions. Maury had never paid the girl much mind. But in tenth grade, when Kera grew titties and an ass, Maury couldn't help but notice his sister's friend.

It wasn't until Tasha and Kera were seniors in high school that she learned that Kera, during sleepovers, would sneak out of her room in the middle of the night to have sex with Maury.

And she never would've known if Kera hadn't ended up sleeping with one of Maury's friends too, which caused Maury and dude to go to blows in gym class. And Maury was suspended.

But he wasn't the only one.

When Tasha found out the reason her brother got suspended, she mopped the math class floor with Kera and was suspended too. She felt that Kera had just been using her, and if nothing else,

Tasha hated the feeling of being used. Ironically, she never felt she was being used by Manolo, since that was a game she got herself into.

Looking at how Maury was feeling Halleigh didn't upset Tasha, though. She looked at Halleigh like a little sister or something. She knew she was good people, so it didn't bother her that Maury was feeling her girl.

Mimi, on the other hand, harbored jealousy. But right now, she wasn't about to trip over no dick, so she just rolled her eyes and collected her cash from the table.

"Fuck what y'all talking about." Mimi licked her fingers as she counted her dough. "I'm about to go shopping. I can finally throw all this stripper shit away," she said as she left the room.

Tasha collected her cash. "I better go with this bitch to make sure she don't go back to Flint just as broke as she left. You coming, Hal?"

Halleigh knew that she needed new clothes. Everything she owned was cheap and indecent, but she honestly had bigger plans for the money sitting in front of her. She shook her head and replied, "Nah, y'all go ahead. I'm good."

Tasha and Mimi grabbed their purses and headed out to hit the stores, leaving Halleigh and Maury alone in the house.

"Why you didn't go with your girls?" Maury asked Halleigh as they sat on the couch watching television.

"I wanted to, but I need this money. I can't afford to go blow it on clothes and handbags. Not right now. I'm really trying to change how I'm living, you know," she said as she looked up at him.

Her beauty was breathtaking, and Maury just stared at her for a moment. "Let me take you shopping. You don't have to spend none of your cash. Everything's on me."

"I can't let you do that," she answered. Halleigh knew better. No man had ever done anything for her unless he was getting something in return. She'd learned from Mimi that an expensive shopping trip from a guy meant she had to give up the booty, and she wasn't ready to do that.

"Yeah, you can, shorty. You got to let a nigga treat you sometimes." Maury figured spending a couple thousand on Halleigh couldn't hurt his pockets, and he wanted to see her happy. "And I know what you're thinking," he said, reading Halleigh's mind. "No strings attached. I'm not looking for anything from you in return. I just want to show you that there are some decent men out there who know how to treat a lady, and I'm one of them. Ya feel me?"

Halleigh thought for a minute before replying with a nod and a smile on her face. "Yeah, I feel you."

"Good. Now let's dip," Maury ordered.

He took out five stacks and put the rest of his share back in the duffle bag and hid it safely in his bedroom wall safe. He got another duffle bag from his bedroom closet and gave it to Halleigh to put her money in.

Then they headed out the door, Halleigh feeling like Julia Roberts being escorted by Richard Gere in the movie *Pretty Woman*.

Maury took her to Macy's in Manhattan and watched her have a field day in the store. He took her to designer stores that she'd never even heard of before, purchasing her high-end clothes, sparing no expense.

Halleigh was enjoying the time that she spent with Maury. He was attentive and protective. When she was with him, he made her feel safe. He walked beside her, his arm draped securely around her shoulder. She almost forgot about the hell that was her life. He made her feel special and didn't judge her or look down on her for the way her life had turned out.

"Can I ask you a question?" she said as he opened the passenger door for her.

"Go ahead."

"Why are you being so nice to me? I mean, you know everything about me. Things that I can't even see past you've disregarded."

"I don't judge people by the past. What's done is done. You can't change that, Halleigh. You can only look forward and do better in the future." Maury leaned into her and kissed her softly on the forehead before pushing her gently into the car.

Halleigh spent the entire day with Maury, and he showed her everything that New York had to offer. They store-hopped for most of the day and then did an early dinner. He even purchased last-minute theatre tickets for *The Color Purple*.

Halleigh was so impressed with the hustle and bustle of New York City. It was completely different than her hometown, and she enjoyed being away from the grit of Flint.

By the time they arrived home, Halleigh was exhausted.

"Thank you for everything, Maury," she stated

as they stood in the dark foyer. "No one has ever done anything like this for me. I had a really good time with you."

"You deserve it," he replied softly as he touched her face.

She gasped from the warmth of his hands and closed her eyes. Halleigh wasn't ready to be in a relationship, but the way she felt when she was with Maury gave her hope that one day she could be happy.

"Come here," he whispered as he grabbed her hand and pulled her to his room. Maury opened the door.

Halleigh reluctantly followed him inside, her heartbeat increasing with each step she took.

After closing the door behind him, he stepped toward Halleigh. Her body trembled slightly, and he smiled to himself. Even though he knew her past, he still sensed an innocent nature in her. He slid the straps of her summer dress off her shoulders, and the fabric dropped to the floor. He then undressed himself, down to his boxers.

Halleigh's breaths became shallow as he pulled her onto his bed. Against her better judgment, she felt the space between her legs become wet.

"Maury, I can't." Her words came out more like a moan than a whisper.

"I know," he replied.

The feeling of his breath on her earlobe sent shivers down her spine.

He pulled back the covers so that she could put her feet underneath and then lay on his back, pulling her head onto his chest. "Go to sleep, Hal.

I want you to feel me next to you. I'm willing to be here for you when you're ready."

Halleigh found a comfortable space on his chest as her legs intertwined with his, and he kissed the top of her head and wrapped his arms around her. Then they both drifted into a peaceful slumber.

Chapter Eleven

The next day, they headed back to Flint. Mimi and Tasha rode in Tasha's car, while Halleigh rode back with Maury.

"What the fuck is wrong with you?" Tasha asked Mimi, noticing the twisted-up expression on her face.

"Nothing." Mimi stared out of the side mirror at the couple following closely behind them. She cut her eyes, pushed her seat back, and pushed her oversized knock-off Dior glasses up on the bridge of her nose.

Truth be told, Mimi didn't like the fact that Maury and Halleigh were riding back to Flint together. Mimi couldn't understand for the life of her why he hadn't asked her to roll back with him. As a matter of fact, she didn't understand why he had stayed up in Halleigh's face the entire time they'd been in New York. She wondered what Halleigh could possibly have that she didn't. After thinking about it for a minute, she came to a conclusion—*Nothing*.

Mimi sighed. She was sick of Halleigh playing the weak and innocent role, the role that always seemed to make it so that she was the center of attention. *Hell, if it wasn't for her ass, Tasha would have never made a way to get us from up under Manolo. Why'd it take this bitch to make her finally give a shit? I been there selling pussy and getting beat down forever and a day and the bitch ain't never try to do no prison-break type of shit when it came to my ass.*

In Mimi's eyes, with Halleigh all up in Maury's face all the time, it was a wonder he could even breathe. Mimi folded her arms over her chest and thought, *Fuck it. If he wants to ride with her ass, let 'em. But that nigga could have been getting the best blow job in his life while we rode.*

Halleigh had no clue about Mimi's brewing anger toward her. Had she known that Mimi was feeling Maury like that, she would have quickly fell back from the jump—not that she was leaning forward or anything like that.

Early that morning, she and Maury had gotten up to talk, and after expressing her concerns to Maury, he agreed to give her time to get herself together. They both decided that it was best for them to be friends and let their relationship progress naturally instead of forcing it.

Being honest with herself, Halleigh had to admit that she did like Maury. But she knew that she'd made the best decision for herself. She needed some "me time," if ever anybody did.

Maury didn't seem to be upset with Halleigh's wishes, and his behavior toward her didn't change at all. In all actuality, he respected her more. And that same respect he showed her was one of the reasons she liked him so much. No matter what the end brought, Halleigh was sure that Maury would become one of her most valuable friends.

Maury glanced over at Halleigh, who was staring idly out of her window. He knew that Flint was the root of all of her problems and that she wasn't thrilled about returning. He reached over and grabbed her hand and told her, "Everything is gon' be all right."

She looked over at him, giving him a weak smile and a nod. "I know," she replied, but her tone wasn't believable.

The frightened looked in her eyes made him glad that he was accompanying them back to Flint. If anything popped off, he wanted to make sure he was there to have the women's backs.

Maury put in Jay-Z's CD *American Gangster,* and Halleigh reclined her seat, as they followed behind Tasha and Mimi and prepared themselves for the ten-hour drive back to the city of Flint.

The first thing the girls did when they arrived back in Flint was find a place to lay their heads. They eventually planned on checking in on the place they had just days ago called home, the roof Manolo had kept over their heads, but they knew it wasn't safe to rest their heads there.

After checking out two other places that had FOR RENT signs in the windows, the girls managed to rent a three-bedroom apartment on the outskirts of Flint. Spots like that didn't care about credit checks and all that mess. All those slum lords wanted was the cash required to move in. If they had to put you out on the streets and rent to the next, then so be it.

Maury moved into a one-bedroom spot nearby and told Tasha to lay low for another couple days, just to be on the safe side.

Tasha agreed to keep her girls in line for a couple of days. Halleigh wasn't going to be a problem, that she could bet the farm on. Mimi, on the other hand, was back in her element, and Tasha didn't know how long she could keep her still before the desire to go get her hustle on in the old way kicked back in.

It was crucial that the girls stayed out of niggas' radars. Word could easily get back to Manolo that they were out kickin' it, doing them instead of seeing about him. That would be a red flag for sure, and it wouldn't take long after that for Manolo to put two and two together and figure out that they were the ones behind his arrest. If that were to happen, then they would have an entirely new set of problems on their hands.

With Tasha, Halleigh, and Mimi out of harm's way, Maury took the opportunity to familiarize himself with his new surroundings. Riding up and down the city streets, he immediately recognized the mentality of its hoods. He could tell that he was in a city that bred killers.

And he couldn't be more right. Every nigga in Flint had the heart of a lion, and if he didn't, then he had his gun to back him up.

Maury knew that scary dudes were the first ones to reach for their pistols when something popped off; therefore, he would have to be on point, especially being in a town that wasn't his home. Dudes always recognized outsiders, and would often try to test them. He immediately decided that he needed to hook up with a Flint native, and knew exactly who he would go to.

Maury knocked on the door to Tasha's apartment. He needed to get at Mimi because he knew she could feed him the information he needed that would allow him to distinguish between the haves and the have-nots of Flint. Mimi had worked the streets of Flint much longer than Halleigh, and besides that, she was live in the game, so he knew that she knew all the players—the starters and the bench warmers. He knew he'd have to watch her, though, to make sure that she knew when to tone herself down and when to keep quiet about things.

He could just as easily have gone to his sister to get information, but she hadn't been in the streets working them the way both Mimi and Halleigh had. And even though Halleigh had been out there on the grind, she was too low-key. Maury did know that eventually Halleigh's assets would be beneficial too. Since she was low-key, he figured she was the type who just sat back and observed a lot of stuff, so sooner or later he'd need to see Flint through her eyes too. But, for now, he needed to get at Mimi, and soon.

After Maury knocked a couple of times, Halleigh answered the door. She was wearing one of the outfits he had purchased for her. The BCBG jeans and a fitted black turtleneck sweater gave her a mature, classy look.

"Hey," she greeted, a smile instantly forming on her face upon seeing Maury standing there.

"What up, ma?" He responded with a smile of his own. Halleigh was the only chick he knew who could possibly distract him from making money. Her aura attracted him, and when he was in her presence, he was always focused on her.

He leaned in and gave her a hug, trying his best to keep it friendly, as she'd requested. He had to keep his mind on the money if he was going to make the most of his little trip to Flint.

"Come on in." She stepped to the side so he could enter their apartment.

"You good?" he asked her. "You need anything?"

Halleigh laughed and shook her head. "No, I don't need anything. I was actually just on my way out. Tasha's not here." She grabbed her leather Hermes bag. "But she should be back any minute. She just ran to the grocery real quick to pick up a few things."

He looked Halleigh up and down and asked, "Yo, so where you headed, shorty? Matter of fact," Maury said as if a sudden thought had just popped into his head, "why is Tasha's ass even out anyway? I thought I told y'all to stay low. Hell, I could have gone to the damn store for her."

"Chill," Halleigh said, pressing her hands downward as if telling him to calm down. "We have been laying low for the past couple days. And Mimi's here. She's right in her bedroom." Halleigh pointed to the closed door toward the end of the hallway.

"Good. At least somebody has some sense to keep they ass in the house," Maury stated. "There's too much at stake for any fuck-ups. The last thing y'all need is for Manolo to get a whiff of y'all's asses and try to come at y'all."

"That's not going to happen. Tasha made a few calls to a couple of people who keep their ear to the street. There's no word out there about what's up with Manolo. We called the jail. No bail is set, so he probably won't be on the streets for a minute." Halleigh shrugged. "So we figured we can't hide out in this matchbox forever. Besides, I'm just going to grab some lunch right at the little restaurant down the block. Is that all right with you?"

Halleigh could see the hesitant look on Maury's face. He didn't reply.

"What?" Halleigh dropped her arms to her side in defeat. "Since you're so worried, why don't you just come with me?" She hadn't spent any time with Maury since they had come back to Flint. She did miss being around him. She loved his listening ear.

"Yeah, all right." He tossed her the keys to his car and said, "Go on and wait for me in the car. I'll be right out. I need to use the restroom."

"I'm driving," she teased, knowing he would never let her behind the wheel of his Lexus.

"Yeah right, shorty. You know better," he stated as he watched her walk out the door. He turned and hurried down the hall to Mimi's room. He knocked lightly.

Mimi snatched open the door and put her hand on one hip when she saw Maury standing there. He hadn't said two words to her since she had given him head back in New York, and she was furious about all the attention he was giving Halleigh. She wondered when Halleigh had found the time to suck his dick, 'cause obviously she had done something to keep the boy interested in her.

"What up?" Mimi asked with an attitude.

"What's up with you, ma?" Maury asked as he entered the room and closed the door behind him. "I'm just coming to check up on you, make sure you're straight."

Mimi looked him up and down to find any sincerity in his words. Was he just fucking with her mind, trying to come back for seconds, or was he really trying to look out for her? Hoping for the latter, she loosened up. She took her hands off of her hips and crossed her arms across her voluptuous chest.

"I'm good," Mimi told him. "I've been trying to get to know you better, but you've been playing me to the left." She walked toward him and stood directly in front of him. Then she reached between his legs and took hold of his firm penis.

Maury had to admit, Mimi was one of the most aggressive chicks he'd ever met. He wished he wasn't feeling Halleigh so much, because he would definitely twist Mimi out. He thought of Halleigh waiting in the car for him and quickly decided to keep things strictly business with Mimi. He saw potential in Halleigh and didn't want to fuck up his chances with her over Mimi.

He removed Mimi's hands from his body. "Nah, it's not like that. As a matter of fact, I got this business that I need to discuss with you."

"Business?" Mimi's ears stood at attention. She knew business always meant money, so she was more than willing to listen. She put money over dick any day, unless the dick transferred into USD.

"Yeah, business," he repeated. "I want you to show me who out this way is getting it."

Mimi shot back, " 'Getting it,' as in, you're trying to take it from 'em? Or 'getting it,' as in, you're trying to see who the competition is around Flint?"

"You already know what's up, Mimi. Ain't nobody fucking with this dried-up-ass dope game out here. I'm trying to take a nigga for what he got."

"What's in it for me?" Mimi was always down for whatever, but something had to be in it for her, and on top of that, it definitely needed to be worth her while.

Maury knew that he could easily manipulate her into giving him the information without giving her shit, but he decided against it. "I'll give you ten percent of the take," he offered. "You wit' it?"

Although ten percent didn't sound like much, it wasn't in Mimi's nature to turn down any type of profit. She knew that ten percent could mean a lot, as long as she handled her end of the deal right. "Yeah, I'm wit' it," she replied.

"Maury!" Halleigh called from a distance.

Mimi rolled her eyes at the sound of Halleigh's voice vibrating through the house. "Get with me when you get off your leash. I got some information that'll help you," Mimi said dryly. She opened up her bedroom door and let Maury out.

Maury had peeped Mimi's jealousy toward Halleigh a long time ago, but he dismissed it. *I did let her suck my dick and then toss her to the side to get with her girl.* The thought made him chuckle as he met Halleigh in the living room.

Halleigh stood in the doorway, her arms crossed. She asked sweetly, "Was you gon' make me wait all day?"

"You know it ain't like that, ma," he responded. He put his hand on the small of her back and led her out of the house.

Mimi watched from the living room window as Maury opened the car door for Halleigh. She couldn't believe how he tried to play her. *Yeah, nigga, I got some information for you.*

She decided to put Maury up on Malek, make him think that Malek was the biggest kingpin Flint had ever seen. Then, once Halleigh found out about Maury's plans to rob Malek, she would never fuck with him.

Nigga think he just gon' play me. I'ma make sure Hal can't stand the sight of the nigga.

Tasha sat in the styling chair as the stylist worked in her hair. New Attitudes was buzzing with gossip, and everybody was talking about Jamaica Joe's going-away party.

"Yeah, that nigga is out of the game. Word is, he bought a house down South and ain't never coming back," a girl stated as she flipped through a hair magazine. "His party is gon' be jumping. You know everybody gon' come out to show him love."

Tasha smiled to herself as she thought about Jamaica Joe making a clean break from the drug game. They had known each other a long time and at one point meant a great deal to one another. Tasha knew that she would be attending Jamaica Joe's party this weekend. It was time for her to show her face again, to let it be known that she was no longer one of Manolo's hoes.

After getting her hair finished in loose curls, she paid her stylist and prepared to leave.

As Tasha reached the doorway, Keesha entered the salon and made her presence felt by bumping Tasha harshly, causing her to drop her purse onto the floor. "Excuse you," Keesha said as she mean-mugged Tasha.

Tasha told her, "I know you saw me coming out of this mu'fucka. You better watch where the fuck you going. Now pick my shit up."

"No, *you* better check your tone before I tell your little secret," Keesha replied softly.

"Bitch, you better stay in your place." Tasha peered at Keesha in a threatening manner.

"I know about your little set-up, Tasha. You, Mimi, and Halleigh better stay in your places. Y'all bitches treated me like shit when y'all thought you were sitting on top of the world, always looking your nose down on a bitch because she wanted to get down with Manolo. It's funny how the tables turn."

Keesha pushed her luck with her last comment, and Tasha smacked the shit out of her, as if she were her pimp. The girls in the salon abruptly ended their conversations and focused on the scene unfolding before them.

Before Keesha could even react, Tasha grabbed her by the back of her weave and brought her head down onto her knee. Keesha screamed in pain and surprise as Tasha pushed her face into the floor. "Bitch, you better remember who kept your ass. I run shit. You can never be a boss bitch like me," she stated as she pushed her head into the marble floor forcefully.

Tasha stood up, collected her belongings, and straightened her clothes as Keesha rolled on the floor, moaning.

Tasha could hear the laughter and instigating comments break out inside the shop as she stormed out and hopped into her car. She had to get to Halleigh and Mimi. They had a problem to handle.

Halleigh sat across from Maury in Applebee's. They were talking and enjoying each other's company as usual.

"So, what have you been up to these past couple days? I haven't seen you since we got here," Halleigh stated as she picked at her food.

"Nothing important. I've just been getting to know your city."

"You still could've stopped by."

"You sound like a woman who was trying to see her man. You can't have it both ways, Hal. You're the one who said you just wanted to be friends."

"I know, I know, and I do want us to be friends. I just missed you, that's all," she admitted. "I've gotten used to spending so much time with you, and then when we got back here, it just stopped all of a sudden."

"I can see this 'friends thing' is gon' be hard already."

Halleigh laughed loudly at the look of distress on Maury's face. "Is it that hard for you?"

"Don't play, Hal. You know how I feel about you.

You say you're not ready, but when we're together, it feels like this is where you want to be. You'll fuck a nigga head up, if he let you."

Halleigh smiled because of how strongly Maury felt for her. "I'm sorry. You're right. I can't expect you to act like my man if you're not my man," she replied. "That's not fair to you."

Maury shook his head. "You ready?"

Halleigh nodded and then hopped out of the booth, while Maury placed his hand on the small of her back.

"Did you pay the club owner for the party?" Jamaica Joe asked Malek as they pulled into the restaurant parking lot.

"Yeah, I took care of it," Malek replied as he parked his brand-new Lincoln Navigator. "Quit worrying about that mu'fuckin' party, fam. Everything is in line for this weekend."

Jamaica Joe and Malek exited the car and headed into Applebee's.

Halleigh stopped in her tracks as Malek crossed her path.

Malek noticed her, and a sense of jealousy overtook him as he saw her standing so intimately with Maury. He looked Maury up and down, and Maury returned his stare as he checked his hip to make sure he was strapped.

Halleigh's breath caught in her throat as Malek approached.

Maury leaned over and whispered, "You know this nigga?"

Halleigh nodded, but didn't say a word. She

couldn't take her eyes off Malek. He looked so different. He'd put on some weight, and his demeanor was hard. Tears welled up in her eyes as she put her head down and began to walk with Maury past Malek.

Malek reached out and grabbed her hand as she passed. "Hal, can we talk for a minute?" he asked.

Halleigh looked back and forth between Maury and Malek.

Maury thought he recognized Malek from the couple of times he'd seen him on television back in the day. He just looked so different, but Maury still had a hunch that the dude standing before him was Malek Johnson, Halleigh's ex-boyfriend. She'd told Maury a lot about their situation. He leaned down and whispered, "Handle your business, shorty. I'm right in the car if you need me." He squeezed her hand in support and lifted her head with his fingertips before he turned to walk away.

Jamaica Joe nodded his head toward the restaurant. "I'm inside, fam," he told Malek.

Malek nodded, never taking his eyes off Halleigh.

The last time Halleigh had seen Malek, he was down with the nigga that had raped her. Coldness immediately filled her heart. "What, Malek?"

Malek eyed Maury's car. "That's your nigga?"

"You know what, Malek? I don't have time for this. After everything we've been through, that's the first thing you ask me?" Halleigh turned to leave.

"A'ight, a'ight, Hal, wait. You're right. That's not my business." Malek looked at her appearance. The last time he'd seen her, her body was deteriorating from drug use, but now she looked good. She was back to the Halleigh he'd fallen in love with, and although there was a lost look in her eyes, she was still very attractive. She had picked her weight back up and was filling up her designer jeans better than ever. She looked healthy, and had transformed from a beautiful girl to a young woman.

"I see you still fucking around with the niggas that raped me," she stated.

"Look, that's handled already."

Halleigh was silent as she stared at Malek.

"I heard about your nigga, Manolo. You good? You need some money or something?" Malek pulled a wad of cash out of his pockets.

"I don't need your money, Malek. Or your pity. I needed you." A tear fell from her eyes. She quickly brushed it away as she began to walk away.

"Halleigh, I'm trying to be here now," he said, halting her in her step.

"How do you know I want you here now?"

"Look, I know you feeling that nigga." Malek nodded toward Maury's truck. "I know you. I can see it in your face, Hal. But you don't love that nigga the way that you love me. You know what we got. I'm trying to make it work with you."

"I've got to go, Malek," Halleigh whispered. Her heart was beating a mile a minute. Malek was right. She did love him. He did know her, but she didn't know if they could ever get past all of their demons to make a relationship work.

"Can we talk later?" she asked. She knew that they needed to talk, but she needed the right words to say. Right now, she was simply running on emotion.

Malek pulled out a VIP pass to Jamaica Joe's party and handed it to Halleigh. "Come by Celebrations this weekend for Joe's going-away party. Things are about to change in Flint, Hal. The nigga leaving everything to me. We'll do it big Saturday night, and we'll talk later that night. I'm trying to see you, Hal. Don't stand me up."

"I won't," she answered with a weak smile.

"I love you, ma," Malek whispered. "You know I do."

"No, I don't know, Malek. We'll talk later," she replied before walking back to Maury's car.

Halleigh hopped into the car and stared out of the window at Malek. She didn't know what to do regarding him. He had hurt her to the point where she thought she couldn't live without him, but now here he was in her face, confessing his undying love.

"Don't let the nigga break your heart, Halleigh," Maury stated as he started his car and pulled away. "You're too good for that."

Chapter Twelve

Lynch, the leader of the infamous Shotta Boyz, passed the Dutch to Sweets as they sat in the front seat of Lynch's Toyota Camry. The haze of the blunt filled the insides of the car, and the two were beyond high as they plotted their murder game.

"You know that bitch nigga Joe leaving town. The grimy mu'fucka know what he got coming to him. That's why he trying to skip out," Lynch stated. "He's throwing a going- away party down at Celebrations. A nigga like me trying to fall up in there just to light the mu'fucka up, nah mean?"

Sweets knew that Lynch was still out to avenge the death of his brother. Jamaica Joe had shot him at point-blank range a year ago, and Lynch had been trying to see Joe ever since. Jamaica Joe was hard to touch, however. He ran the North Side of Flint and stayed on point at all times. He had an army of young soldiers who were willing to protect him at all costs, making it hard for Lynch to get his revenge.

"Nah, fam, I got that handled. The only thing we got to do is sit back and listen to the gunshots ring out. The nigga Joe ain't ever gon' make it out of Flint. Him and his li'l nigga Malek gon' meet death that night." A smile crossed Sweets' face. He hit the blunt and held the smoke down in his lungs before passing it back to Lynch.

"Fuck you got doing the job? You know ain't a nigga in Flint who can put they murder game down better than your boy."

"That's why I got a bitch doing it."

"Whaat?" Lynch exclaimed in disbelief. "You's a lyin' mu'fucka." He shook his head.

"No bullshit, my nigga. They'll never see her coming. Like I said before, it's curtains for the North Side and anybody who affiliated with 'em."

Lynch nodded his head. His focus was taken off the conversation when he noticed a short, light-skinned girl with curly hair approach Sweets' home. He tapped Sweets. "Ain't that the bartender bitch from Manolo's spot?"

Sweets peered through the window. "Yeah, that's her. Fuck is she doing?" he wondered as she knocked on his door. "How the fuck this bitch know where I live?"

Sweets rolled down his window, releasing clouds of haze into the sky. "You looking for something?"

When Keesha turned around and looked at him, he could see that there was a long gash across her forehead. He frowned at the sight. *Somebody fucked this bitch up,* he thought.

"Yeah, I need to talk to you," Keesha replied.

Sweets shook his head, figuring she wanted money or a place to stay. Manolo had only been locked up for a couple of weeks, but many of his hoes had come to Sweets looking for help. They figured, since Sweets and Manolo were partners, that Sweets would take them in. Sweets didn't bother with Manolo's bitches and only took a cut of their earnings. He could give a fuck if they were out on the streets.

"I ain't got nothing for you." Sweets hit the button to roll up his window.

"Wait!" Keesha approached his side of the car.

"Bitch is persistent." Lynch chuckled at Sweets' irritated expression.

"What?"

Keesha said quickly, "I got some information about why Manolo's club was raided."

Sweets immediately changed his tune. "I'm listening."

"Tasha, Mimi, and Halleigh went to the police and told them what Manolo had in his safe. After the raid, they met with the lead detective and split the bricks and the money. That's why nobody's seen their faces since it happened."

Sweets shook his head. "I don't know where you got your information from, but somebody told you wrong. Don't come around my block looking for me again unless you got something important to say."

A look of confusion spread across Keesha's face as she watched Sweets roll his window up and disappear behind the dark tint.

"How the fuck you just gon' pass on that valuable shit she just told you, fam?" Lynch asked, an annoyed look on his face. "The bitch info might be legit."

"It was legit. I just didn't want the bitch to think I owe her something for putting me up on game. That's why I don't fuck with these bitches. You can't trust 'em. I took a loss when the police confiscated what was in Manolo's safe. I'm gon' take care of them bitches . . . right after I take care of Jamaica Joe."

Chapter Thirteen

It was Friday night and Celebrations was jumping. Everyone from the North Side came out to celebrate with Jamaica Joe. The huge parking lot was filled to capacity, as cars continued to pile in. Sweets sat in his truck toward the back of the lot, along with the Shottah Boyz. He couldn't believe Jamaica Joe had practically delivered himself on a silver platter by throwing this party. Sweets had been lying low for the past couple of months, just waiting for Joe to resurface. And now here he was.

Ain't this nigga learned his lesson about throwing parties? Sweets thought. He shook his head. He said to his crew, "This nigga must've thought the beef was dead. He slippin' like a mu'fucka. He honestly believes that he can throw a big party without having to see me?" Sweets laughed and then cocked his automatic 9 millimeter pistol. "He got another thing coming."

Lynch, the oldest of the Shottah Boyz, asked, "So, we just busting in there shooting?"

"Nah, nah, that ain't smart. We going to clear that mu'fucka out, and then I got it from there. It's all taken care of. Tonight the North Side gon' feel Sweets, believe that!"

"So, we're just going to wet the whole place up? How are we going to get to Jamaica Joe? It's not going to be that easy."

"We're just going to cause a diversion to put my plan into motion. That's only the beginning, my nigga. Jamaica Joe and that li'l nigga Malek are dying tonight. That's my word," Sweets said boldly.

That comment was music to Lynch's ears. He'd wanted Jamaica Joe dead for some time now. Joe was responsible for the shooting death of Lynch's youngest brother, so Lynch was out for blood. Jamaica Joe gave them the perfect opportunity to strike back by having this big party.

"This is for Rah-Rah," Sweets said as he pushed PLAY on his dashboard TV. A homosexual porno began to play on the screen.

The Shottah Boyz hated it, and didn't approve of Sweets' sexual orientation, but they couldn't do anything because Sweets was the boss. They tried their best to avoid looking at the screen, but still, the sounds were almost too much to bear.

Lynch frowned. "Sweets, man, why can't you turn that gay shit off?"

Sweets didn't even acknowledge his henchman's comment. He just sat back and rested his hand on his gun, a small smile spread across his face.

It was the middle of August, but Sweets and the

Shottah Boyz were about to make it look like the Fourth of July.

Jamaica Joe and Malek walked through the back entrance of the club, surrounded by their whole crew. They were draped in all black, and everyone was shining with long platinum Jesus pieces and crosses. Joe wore a black linen shirt and Armani slacks, with none other than Stacy Adams gators on his feet. Joe was the only one who wasn't sportin' any jewels. He only wore a watch, which spoke for itself, since his watch cost more than all his henchmen's jewels put together.

Malek didn't wear any jewelry either. Joe taught him that conservative is always better, so he took heed and did away with the flashy jewelry. Malek just rocked an all-black hoodie under a black Sean John leather jacket, his burner tucked in the front pockets. An oversized fitted cap covered his eyes, and the only facial features that could be seen were his perfect white teeth and his neatly lined goatee.

The crew mobbed into the club, and they could hear the new Lil' Wayne song that had been blasting the airwaves, with all of the radio play it had been getting in Flint. Jamaica Joe, Malek, and their crew made their presence known. Joe's henchmen began to make it rain on their way up to the VIP section. The club went crazy at the sight of them entering the club. It was a fitting send-off for Joe.

Malek couldn't help but glance around in

search of Halleigh. He had a lot of things he needed to say to her, things she hadn't given him a chance to say before. He hoped that they could heal old wounds and make amends. This time, no matter what, he was determined to get the love of his life back once and for all.

Chapter Fourteen

Tasha, Mimi, and Halleigh pulled up to the club, Foxy Brown blasting out of the speakers. They were all dressed to impress that night, determined to be the showstoppers of the party.

"Damn! It's jumping in there," Mimi said as she examined the people lining up to get in the club.

"I told you it was going to be popping," Tasha said as she maneuvered her car up to the valet.

Halleigh was consumed by her own thoughts. *I hope Malek is in there. I really need to see him. I miss that boy so much.* Halleigh had been looking forward to running into Malek ever since Tasha had told her about the party. Even though a part of her couldn't understand why he was hanging with one of the men that raped her, she knew deep down inside that she had to give him the benefit of the doubt. There was a chance that he'd had no idea that was the man who'd raped her. By the same token, Malek could have very well known, and was secretly plotting his own revenge. Halleigh hoped for the latter.

So many things went unsaid between her and Malek, and truth be told, Halleigh wanted to see if their love was still there. Hopefully, tonight would be her chance.

As the three women hopped out of the car, all eyes were on them. Everyone expected to see Manolo close behind, but to their surprise, he was nowhere in sight. All of the girls strutted in with a model's precision and went straight to the VIP line so that they could avoid waiting. It was double the admission price, but they were coming in with style.

Maury sat outside in his rental car, waiting for his plan to come into play. He'd rented a motel room two buildings down from the club and was about to show Flint how New York niggas got down. He just hoped that Mimi didn't back out on him. *I shoulda fucked her to get her head gone first,* Maury thought as he watched the people fill up the club. He wasn't sure if Mimi was as bold as she claimed to be.

He looked toward the valet and saw his sister, Mimi, and Halleigh hop out of the car, all of them wearing diva shades. When Mimi got out, she pulled her shades down slightly and looked over her rims toward the building where Maury was. The two of them locked eyes, and she nodded her head, signaling to him that the plan was still in motion.

Maury then looked over at an unknowing Halleigh and his eyes got stuck. She was so beautiful. The dress she wore hugged her curves, and the high heels enhanced her long, toned legs. Maury's joint began to harden just at the sight of her. He quickly snapped out his brief daydream and refocused. He, too, needed for his head to be right in order for everything to go down as planned.

Halleigh entered the club along with her girls. She noticed a lot of commotion coming from the rear of the club and tried to get a peep of what was going down. A blizzard of money was being tossed in the air, and the women in the club were going crazy, scrambling for the free cash. A mob of gentlemen dressed in all-black began parting the crowd like God parted the Red Sea for Moses.

Halleigh stood on her tippy-toes, trying to get a better view. "Damn! Who is that?"

"Yo, that's Jamaica Joe and them," Tasha said, a smile spread across her face. She had history with Joe and was going to make it a point to see him before the night was over.

The girls made their way over to a table near the bar and settled.

"It's jumping in this mu'fucka." Mimi danced to the music while still in her chair. "Where the mu'-fuckin' ballers at?"

"You know all the broke niggas are on the main floor. What we need to be doing is getting into VIP." Tasha waved over the waiter.

Halleigh looked at the group of men going up the wraparound stairs that led to the VIP section. As she took a closer look, she noticed Malek was ahead of the pack, and her heart fluttered at the sight of him.

Tasha noticed Halleigh's attention was focused on something or someone. Tasha's eyes shot to the crew also, and her vision fixed on Jamaica Joe.

Jamaica Joe is looking good tonight. She licked her lips and fixed her freak-'em dress.

Mimi looked at the entourage. She had a totally different agenda than her friends. She wanted to get the attention of the biggest baller in the club so she could put her plan into motion.

She downed her rum and Coke and stood up. "Let's see if we can we get up in VIP, where the real party is at."

"That's what's up." Halleigh stood up alongside Mimi.

All the girls made their way to the VIP section, each with their own personal agenda.

Chapter Fifteen

"This toast is to celebrate our family, a family of hustlers, a family of brothers. Flint is ours. No, fuck that, the world is ours!" Jamaica Joe held up a wine glass along with the other ten men in the room, including Malek.

"The world is ours," they all said in unison as they tapped their glasses and downed the Moet.

Malek smiled, but then it quickly disappeared at the thought of what he had become. He looked around and noticed he was in the midst of killers and hustlers, something his deceased mother and stepfather had forbid him to become. Everything in his life seemed to happen so quickly that he couldn't even remember changing into the person he was today.

Making his way away from the crowd, Malek walked over to the window that overlooked the main floor and noticed a group of women maneuvering through the crowd. He smiled as he saw Halleigh, looking beautiful, on her way up to VIP.

"There my girl go," he said. He gripped the Moët bottle by its neck and took another swig.

Moments later, Tasha, Mimi, and Halleigh made their way to VIP, and after being searched by one of the bouncers, they were let in. Immediately after entering the room, the girls noticed the more relaxed environment that the VIP offered. Nice, slow music was playing and the oval, over-sized couches were full with people relaxing and drinking.

Halleigh and Malek were instantly drawn to one another. They locked eyes, and it seemed as if there was no one else in the room but them. They slowly walked toward each other, neither trying to seem too anxious. As they neared each other, Halleigh smiled, and Malek returned the gesture. They stood face to face, staring at each other, not knowing what to say.

"I miss you," Halleigh said.

"I miss you like crazy too," Malek replied.

The two kind of chuckled and then embraced. Just the three little words, *I miss you*, were the beginning of the mending of their relationship. So many words had danced through each of their minds about what they would say to each other once they met up again, but none of those words even mattered now. Everything was like water under the bridge.

Malek and Halleigh, still embracing each other, slowly rocked back and forth. The warmth of Malek's body and embrace felt so good to Halleigh. Malek led her toward the back, and they sat on the couch.

Halleigh looked closely at Malek and noticed a

lot had changed with him. It was the first time she'd noticed the tattoo on his neck. It had the name of his deceased mother, and on his forearm, the words *North Side* were embedded in his skin.

"You're all tatted up now, huh?" She gave him a sexy grin.

Malek looked down at his forearm and then back at Halleigh. "Yeah, a li'l somethin'-somethin'," he said softly, smiling back at her. "Look, Halleigh, I gotta be honest. I'm still in love with you, and I think about you constantly, nah mean?"

"I feel the same way, Malek. I don't want to play games. I want to be for real with you, and my love for you is real. It always has been. You know that. And us being apart—"

"Look, I can't take this no more either, Halleigh. You supposed to be with me, girl." Malek grabbed her hand and looked deep into her brown eyes.

Halleigh had been waiting to hear those words come out of Malek's mouth for a very long time. She'd dreamed of hearing those words, and now her dream was becoming a reality. Under the control of Manolo, Halleigh wasn't able to be with her love, but with Manolo now out of the picture, she was ready to be where she belonged. "I want to be with you too, Malek."

"We've wasted enough time, Hal. A lot of things are going to change. I'm coming into big things right now, and I want you to be a part of it."

"What do you mean?"

"I want you to be my woman. I want us to look forward and forget about the past."

"Are you serious?"

"I'm dead serious. We've wasted enough time. The life you living is not for you. Let me take care of you. I'm about to be over all of this." Malek waved his hand over the room.

A confused Halleigh asked, "All of what? This club?"

"No," Malek corrected her, "this whole side of town." He looked around again. "The North Side is mine, baby." He looked into Halleigh's eyes. "It's ours."

Halleigh had to make sure she was hearing him correctly. "You taking over for Jamaica Joe?"

Malek nodded his head humbly. Now that he had Halleigh's attention, he wasn't going to let her slip away. He was ready to make her his main woman, and he wasn't taking no for an answer.

Tears started to form in Halleigh's eyes. Tears of joy. Halleigh had waited so long to be at that point with Malek. She'd finally linked back up with her soul mate and wasn't going to squander the chance. "Okay. Promise to always take care of me." Halleigh inched closer to Malek.

"I promise."

They embraced each other.

Malek wasted no time. He instructed her to go home and pack her stuff so she could be with him. He knew that she'd been through a lot. He didn't care what she'd done in her life before that point. From that moment on, she was his woman.

Halleigh asked, "What am I supposed to do about my girls? I came here with them."

"It's me and you against the world. You have to leave that lifestyle alone and turn over a new leaf. How about this? After I handle a little business, I will book us a vacation, so we can start this off right."

"Are you for real?" Halleigh said excitedly.

Malek nodded his head. "I always told you that I would take you away from Flint, didn't I? Even if it is just for a moment. A promise is a promise, right?" Malek smiled.

"Right." Halleigh smiled back.

Malek went into his pocket and pulled out a wad of money, nothing but large faces. "Go home and get your things. I will meet up with you after I drop Joe off at the airport." Malek gave Halleigh his cell phone number.

Halleigh couldn't believe everything that was happening to her right now. It was as if a prince had come and swept her off her feet. Manolo had treated her so bad, she forgot how it felt to have a man's love, but she was witnessing it firsthand.

Without even saying a word to Mimi and Tasha, Halleigh crept out the back of the club along with Malek. He walked to the curb and hailed a cab for her.

"Go 'head and get your things and wait for me. I will have one of my boys bring me to you." Malek opened up the cab door for her.

"Okay," Halleigh said as she got in.

"It's me and you against the world. I'm coming for you."

"I love you, Malek Johnson."

Malek smiled and closed the door for her. After he dropped Jamaica Joe off, he was going to get his woman. It was their time now.

Chapter Sixteen

While Tasha was drinking and mingling, Mimi was doing just the opposite. She was playing the back, trying to see who had the deepest pockets so she could lure them to Maury. She watched as Tasha became the center of attention, and it was obvious that she was well known and respected. The men gave Tasha respect. They weren't on her like vultures, and all seemed to be just enjoying her company.

Mimi looked around for Halleigh and didn't see her. She then looked around for Malek and didn't notice him either. *They must have ducked out for a minute,* she thought as she continued to scan the VIP room.

Jamaica Joe sat at the bar, talking to a fair-skinned woman with green eyes. She was by far the most beautiful woman up in the club, if not the city of Flint. Her island accent only added to her sexiness. They had been engrossed in deep conversation for the past hour. He'd just met her that night, and they clicked. Although the woman had a good conversation game, Joe was trying to see her without them clothes on. He sat talking to her, scoping her whole body out and stopping at her inner thighs. Her dress had risen up, slightly revealing her red lace panties

"You're a bad boy," the woman said in a sexy voice. "I see your eyes wandering down there."

"I'm sorry, but I can't help but look. You are a beautiful woman."

"Well, maybe we should go somewhere private after the party to show you how beautiful I really am." She licked her lips seductively.

Joe's manhood began to jump instantly at the sexy woman's advance. He hated that he had a flight out of town later that night. He wanted nothing more than to take her up on her offer, leave with her right then and there, but then he thought, *I can't leave my own party.* "I have plans tonight, but we will get it in soon." He couldn't believe what he was saying as he looked her up and down again.

He watched as she spread her legs, causing her dress to come up higher and expose her vagina.

"Very soon," he added, his manhood rock-hard.

"Well, let me just give you a little something to tide you over until you can find the time for me, *papi.*" The woman stood up and began to sway her hips to the music.

Joe watched as the mystery woman seductively danced to a slow rhythm. He was totally in a trance. He didn't know if it was the liquor or his imagination, but she was looking more like a goddess than just a beautiful woman. She slowly wound her ass up against his now erect penis and was giving him a lap dance while he sat comfortably on the club's loveseat. He looked around for Malek and noticed that he had left the VIP section. *Where my nigga at?* He frowned up, but quickly focused back on the fat backside of the mystery woman.

Malek returned inside the club with Halleigh on his mind. He was ready to make it work for them. His entire life seemed to be about new beginnings right now. He thought about the sudden change in his life. He was about to become the boss, and he had finally gotten his woman back. He maneuvered through the packed club, trying to reach the VIP section. That's when he bumped into Mimi.

"Malek, what's good?" Mimi rested her hand on his chest.

"What's up with you? Cece, right?" Malek asked, trying to recall Mimi's name.

"No, boy! You know my name is Mimi." She playfully hit him, one hand on her hip.

Malek wasn't really trying to make small talk, so he smiled and began to walk away. But before he could leave, he felt her grab his arm. He turned back toward her to see what she wanted.

"I need to holla at you about something," she yelled, trying to be heard over the loud music.

"Maybe later." Malek freed his arm and began to leave.

Mimi knew she had to act fast if her plan was to go smoothly, so she said the first thing that came to mind that she thought would catch his attention.

"It's about Halleigh. Someone is trying to kill her!" she blurted out, staring at Malek, hoping he would go for it.

"What?" he said as he frowned up and got closer to hear her better.

Mimi was smiling inside. She knew he'd taken her bait. "Let's go over here and talk." She grabbed his hand and led him to an empty table.

They sat down, and Mimi began to work her improvisation skills. She knew that Maury was outside waiting for her to bring a victim out so he could get them. Maury had told her to find a "get-money" nigga and he would handle the rest, explaining to her that he would kill whoever she put him on, so retaliation wasn't a worry for her.

She saw Malek as prey. *Why not get the next nigga in charge? This game ain't fair, and I'm out for self.* She waved the waiter over to their table. "Gimme two shots of Patron," she said, then focused her attention back to Malek.

"What the fuck are you talking about?" Malek asked.

"Well, it's this nigga that Halleigh used to trick with." Mimi paused and grabbed the drinks the waiter was handing to her. "One of her old tricks, he is after her. Malek, I think he's gonna kill her. He's nuts."

"What? Who?" Malek asked, growing more enraged at the sound of someone bringing harm to Halleigh. He had made a vow that he would never allow anyone to hurt her again, not under his watch.

Malek was so busy trying to figure out what was going on that he didn't see Mimi drop the crushed-up Ecstasy pills into his drink. She discreetly shook it up to hide the substance.

"Here, take a drink. You need one for what I'm about to tell you," Mimi said, hoping that he would follow her instructions. She turned her head to make sure no one was keeping an eye on them, and by the time she turned back around, Malek had downed the drink and was wiping his mouth.

Malek, wanting to know more about this person trying to harm Halleigh, wiped his mouth and focused back on Mimi. "What the fuck are you talking about? Who got a beef with Halleigh?"

I got 'im, Mimi thought as she made up a false story.

Maury sat outside in the car, patiently waiting for Mimi to come out of the club with a victim. *This bitch bullshitting. I hope she don't back out.* He took a puff of the weed-filled blunt that hung out of his mouth. He saw the cars and bling that the men had on as they were coming in and out of the club, and he was like a fat kid at the candy store.

"I'm about to shake this mu'fucka up. Word to my mother!" he said to himself as he smiled sinisterly. Just as he finished his sentence, he saw Mimi coming out of the club with a man who seemed to be drunk.

"Bingo!" he said as he realized that Mimi had come through for him. *That's the nigga that Halleigh bumped into the other day,* he thought.

He knew that he'd hit the jackpot, because on that day, he saw that Malek was driving a Range

Rover, one of the more expensive luxury SUVs. He also knew from the way the man was staggering that Mimi had slipped him the pills that he'd supplied her. He knew that a man with a hard dick and a blurred thought process was easy money. He just hoped that this nigga was a real baller and not some wannabe flashy punk, so he could lead him to a stash spot. Maury was a professional at what he did and was ready to introduce Flint to his honed craft.

Maury started up his vehicle and watched. Mimi had her arm around the man's waist as he openly groped her breasts. They walked two buildings down to the motel that Maury had booked earlier that day. He pulled the vehicle into the parking lot of the motel as Mimi practically dragged Malek into the room.

He cocked his pistol and caught a hard-on, something that happened every time he was about to hit a caper. "Let's get it," he whispered as he exited the car with a rolled-up ski mask on top of his head.

Chapter Seventeen

Sweets and the Shottah Boyz loaded up the clips to their pistols and prepared to make it rain bullets inside the club where Joe and the North Side crew were getting their party on. They approached the door, which was guarded by only one of Joe's henchmen. Before the henchman realized who was approaching him, Lynch sent a hollow-tip slug through his forehead, killing him instantly. They made their way into the club, about to set it off.

Boom! Boom! Boom!

Shots rang out one after another and sent Celebrations into complete pandemonium. Joe, by habit, reached for his pistol and got low. He pulled the mystery woman to the floor with him, and then everyone in the VIP followed suit.

Sweets and the Shottah Boyz stood in the middle of the club, letting their assault rifles go off. They weren't aiming at anyone in particular. They just shot at the ceiling to try to lure Jamaica Joe out of the building, so their scheme would succeed.

Joe looked onto the main floor and saw Sweets and his crew letting off rounds. "Yo, go get at them niggas!" he said as he grabbed the girl and ran to the private entrance through the back of the club. He had routed a getaway path just in case something like this went down. The woman Joe was with gripped his hand as he led her to his truck, which was parked in the back right by the door.

Chapter Eighteen

Mimi watched as Malek clumsily stumbled onto the motel's bed and lay flat on his back. He gripped his rock-hard dick and Mimi almost felt sorry for him. She knew that Maury would kill him after he got him to take him to his stash spot, but greed pushed her to let the scene unfold. She seductively walked over to Malek and dropped to her knees. She then began to unbutton his Evisu jeans as he tried to pull away.

"What you doing, ma?' he said almost incoherently, slurring each syllable.

"Just relax, Malek. Your mouth is saying no, but your friend down here is saying yes," Mimi said just before she took Malek's ten inches into her mouth.

She had purposely left the door unlocked so Maury could creep in. *Where this nigga at? He's taking all day,* she thought as she continued to go up and down on Malek's shaft. She grabbed his rock-hard pipe and began playing with the tip of it with her tongue.

She paused to look at Malek, and as she looked

up, what she saw scared the living shit out of her. Malek was smiling with his pistol in his hand. His demeanor had totally changed. He no longer looked distraught and confused, like he had been moments before.

"You look surprised," Malek said just before he struck her in the temple, causing her to fly onto the motel's carpeted floor.

She gripped her bloody forehead in agony, and her vision became temporarily blurred.

"You thought I didn't see you try to slip me that spiked drink, ma? Huh? I ain't new to this, I'm true to this!" Malek yelled as he stood up and put his pipe back in his jeans.

Only moments before he'd pretended to drink the spiked liquor, but had quickly poured it on the floor when Mimi's head was turned.

He pointed his gun at Mimi. "Now look at you! That's why niggas can't trust these hoes out here! I know a nigga is about to come in here any second now. I saw yo' dumb ass leave the lock unlocked, and I peeped you scoping out that blue car that followed us in here."

"Malek, wait! I—"

Malek struck her again in the head with the butt of the gun. He aimed the gun at Mimi's head. "Who is trying to hurt Halleigh? Were you telling the truth?"

Mimi, scared to lie, tried to tell the truth. "No, it was a—"

Before Mimi could get out her sentence, Malek sent a hollow-tip through her chest with his silenced pistol. He heard all he needed to hear.

To his surprise, he wasn't even afraid of catching his second body. The rage inside of him made the situation easier. Now his only concern was the guy that was scheduled to come in the room any second.

Halleigh couldn't wipe the smile off of her face if she wanted to. She was so happy about Malek's proposition, and she couldn't wait to move forward and leave her current lifestyle in the dust. She rummaged through her clothes, trying to stuff all she could into her luggage. Malek had made her feel like a new woman, and she couldn't wait to start her life with him.

It only took her thirty minutes to pack up everything. She called Malek's cell, but he didn't pick up, so she left a message that she was ready and told him where he could pick her up. She then sat on the porch, waiting for her Prince Charming to arrive. *Hurry up and get here, Malek,* she thought as she waited anxiously.

Malek stood over Maury's shaking body as he watched him struggle for his life. Malek had caught him with four slugs to the chest the moment he walked through the motel door.

Malek held the smoking gun in his hand and began to tremble slightly. In his twenty years on earth, he had never killed anyone, but now in the past couple of weeks, he had caught three bodies.

He witnessed Maury take his last breath and then quickly fled the scene. He ran over to the club to put Joe on to what had happened.

For all Malek knew, Sweets had set this whole thing up as an attempt to take him out. On the other hand, it could have just been Mimi trying to set him up on her own. But either way it went, he needed to confide in his mentor. If Sweets was setting Malek up for the okey-doke, then chances were he was setting Joe up too. Malek had to warn him.

Malek's heart pounded frantically as he raced to the back entrance of the club. He noticed the large group of people running out of the club in a frenzy, and then he found out why. He heard the gunfire coming from the club and quickly gripped his pistol tighter. He ran to the back entrance, where he knew Joe would be coming out. He spotted Joe's car and then he saw Joe and the young lady he was with earlier jump into it.

"Joe!" Malek yelled as he ran to the truck.

"Come on, Malek. Jump in!" Joe screamed as he waved Malek over.

The girl took the back seat, and Malek jumped into the passenger's side.

"Joe," Malek said, nearly out of breath, "a nigga tried to set me up in the—"

Before he could say anything, the girl reached into her garter belt and pulled out a snub-nosed .22 pistol. She let off a shot to the back of Joe's head and then reached over and shot Malek three times to the chest. Joe's limp head rested on his horn, causing it to honk continuously, blood covering the front window.

The girl that Sweets had sent for the job smiled. She loved what she did because she was damn good at it. She was one of the most prolific hit-hoes in the underground world. She could get to dons quicker than anyone could even fathom.

Just as she was about to step out of the car to meet Sweets in the front as he had instructed, a phone rang. It was Malek's cell.

"Hello?" the mystery woman said, trying to add salt to the wound. She always did menacing things like that. She got an adrenaline rush and laughter out of her bold, sinister act.

"Who is this? Where is Malek?" the female voice on the other end of the phone asked.

"He's sleeping," she said before letting out a big laugh and hanging up. She left the car, leaving Joe and Malek slumped.

After fifteen minutes of waiting on Malek to pick her up, Halleigh tried calling him on his cell phone again, but when a woman picked up and told her that he was sleeping, she was dumbfounded. She just looked at her phone in disbelief. Her heart crumbled at the thought that another woman had picked up Malek's phone. He was supposed to be on his way to pick her up and yet he was with another woman.

I knew it was too good to be true. I knew it, Halleigh thought. Tears began to flow down her cheeks. Once again, her heart had been broken in two.

THE END
(of *FLINT* book 3)

. . . but the saga continues in *FLINT* book 4.